CINDERBLOCK HOUSES

CINDERBLOCK HOUSES

A Collection of Short Stories by

KRISTA CREEL

BOOKS

Adelaide Books

New York / Lisbon

2018

Cinderblock Houses
a collection of short stories
by Krista Creel

Published by Adelaide Books, New York / Lisbon
An imprint of the Istina Group DBA
adelaidebooks.org

Editor-in-Chief
Stevan V. Nikolic

For any information, please address Adelaide Books
at info@adelaidebooks.org

ISBN13: 978-0-9996451-4-7
ISBN10: 0-9996451-4-5

Printed in the United States of America

For John

Contents

Bent Broke

We had some work to get done at the Buckalews. They lived a mile down the road on the rich end of Feathers Chapel in a big, stone house with a blue-eyed dog. I had never seen a blue-eyed dog before, and I was almost afraid to stare straight at him. Looked like devil eyes to me. But he smelled like baby powder so I figured he was ok.

My dog, Pip, was Chihuahua mixed with German shepherd. Sharla said that was impossible, like one of our hens nesting with a turkey buzzard, but I know Pip's part German shepherd. Pip knows it too. He's very protective like one. Follows me everywhere.

Sometimes it's good being followed because it means you're worth following; other times, it's not so good, like when the truancy officer follows you home.

I had a one-eyed cat that would follow me and Welby into the woods when we'd hunt until one day she peed in the corn he had put out to trick the deer, and Welby got fed up. (He was always fed up about something. It never made sense to me, being fed up. It sounded like you were stuffed with grits and they were coming back up and that's what made you so ornery.) Anyway, Welby shot at her. He had to. Most people hunt for fun, but we hunt for jerky and stew. He had a clear shot, but he missed. I'm sure it's because that cat's name was Lucky because Welby never missed a shot, and he'd never admit to being soft. I never saw her again after that, though. We got a doe the next day.

It was a windy out. The tarp flapped over the wood stack, and the metal door to the shed knocked against itself. Wind never bothered me. It seemed to part around me as if I was at the bottom of Moses' Red Sea.

I climbed up on the fender of Welby's tractor. It was a big, old tractor. It had been the gravedigger at Peebles Cemetery until Welby bought it off them. They got a new one around the same time they got their new Cadillacs. Business must be good for the undertakers. Just last week Eric Jensen was crushed in the cotton combine. Before that, it was Mrs. Rosaleigh Dunn. She just died of old age, but it was a couple of days before they found her.

All I can say is when I die I hope I get to ride in one of those shiny, black Cadillacs. People will look at me as I pass by and nod and say I was something special.

Welby kept the gravedigger together with odd parts. It was rusted in places and painted in others with a busted headlight and noisy engine. But no matter what he put that tractor through and no matter how many times it stalled or stuck, he got it running again.

"It ain't the look of things," he would say. "It's the guts that matter."

The guts to his tractor were made up of whatever he could construct of clothes hangers, duct tape and metal parts.

He jumped up on the seat and turned the key. It kicked on like some tired, hot bull. The fender rumbled and smoke shot out of the exhaust pipe, and we began the treacherous event of getting out of the driveway. It was clay gravel with lots of holes that would catch the rainwater and wash out, no matter how many times we filled them or what with— grass clippings, chicken bones, ceramic pots. Nothing stayed in those holes for long. So, whatever we took down it, that driveway would shake us fierce. This time, it shook a moth out of my ear, I swear. I saw it fly up into the catalpa tree and laugh at me.

Feathers Chapel Road was an improvement from our driveway, but it was bumpy, too, from the new patches of asphalt that the workers from the penal farm filled in last week. Seems to me the jailers should give those inmates something more productive to do, if the roads are just as bumpy with fixed holes as without. I try to accomplish something productive every day, no matter if it is just getting out of the driveway or shaking a moth loose.

Pip was trying to follow us, like always, so I had to kick at him. It was for his own good. He was a danger to himself, catapulting off the wheels of the tractor like a grasshopper, which is why grasshoppers get squished or end up stuck in the grills of Mack trucks.

Once we got out, Welby straddled the road and the ditch to let cars pass. I hung onto the fender with one hand and picked kudzu off the trees with the other. He would've put on his blinkers if he had had any that worked. The caution sign on the back was holed with buckshot.

I waved at the Washingtons as we passed. They were playing dominoes under a tent. They were always very quiet about it, not paying me any mind. Parker Washington was fresh from jail. He wasn't much older than me. I don't know what he did. Welby knew but he wouldn't tell me.

We passed Nettle hanging laundry. She had her baby in a sling around her belly. She was three months behind on her bills. She had lost her job at the nursing home—accused of taking a ring from an old lady. Now she might lose her house. She's what Welby calls bent broke. We were all behind, but she was sooner to serious.

The Mennonites were putting out their spring mums for sale. Their yard was always clean and their cows fat. I felt sorry for the girls though, wearing dresses all day, even on four-wheelers. Didn't make much sense to me.

I had a dress once, but I outgrew it.

The air was filled with the smell of wild onions and daffodils and wet purple clover, and then there was the dryer sheets and fresh manure and loblollies. Gobs of loblollies broke from the hard freeze we had just had a couple weeks back. Their tops had been pushed from the road and into the ditch like trash. One tree bent all the way over the road, and an ugly, old crow sat on it like it was holding it down. Momma had always said that sometimes the smallest things could hold you down, so when that bird flew away I thought that tree would spring right back up. But it didn't.

The needles rustled up my hair as we rode under it.

One time Welby cut off all the branches of the big gum tree behind our house. It wasn't good to put gum in the potbelly, but it was all we had that winter, so he had to do it. It was my favorite climbing tree, and I would've sacrificed warm hands for it. I had given up more for less. Besides, I stayed all winter long under great-grandma Jesse's quilt anyway.

I prayed hard that the tree wouldn't die or that at least another would spring up in its place. And can you believe it? All those limbs grew back the very next summer. They reminded me of those toothpicks we stuck in potatoes in science class and put in a paper cup with water until they sprouted. They weren't the strong climbing limbs that they used to be, but they were a start.

Welby says prayers don't work, I prayed again anyway, this time for momma to come home.

Welby's my daddy, if you want to know, but not my real daddy. I never met him. I asked Welby once if I could just call him Daddy, but he said no. He said it made him feel responsible for me, even though, according to the courts, he was responsible for me. But he didn't have to be. We weren't blood. Sometimes he'd go off and not come back for a while. Sharla said those casinos in Mississippi had a hold of him. She said they float on water like giant, glittering barges, so I didn't blame him for leaving and wanting to stay left. They were probably anchored to a big pot of money down in the muddy bottoms that giant alligator turtles snapped at and catfish guarded with their barbs.

That's probably why Welby's hand was all cut up. He had wrapped it in one of my momma's old scarves and tied it in a knot above his knuckles. His blood made flowers on the rag like wild roses. I would've asked him what happened, but he would've said to keep to my own business. I knew he was a go-getter, so he probably tried to get that pot of money, just like that one time I saw him go and get a pump off the neighbor's diesel tank.

"You gotta take what you want," he would say. "Ain't nobody gonna give you nothing."

He was smart like that, but the neighbor didn't think so. He took the pump back and raised a pistol at him. We're not allowed on his property anymore, not that I want to get on it anyway. Only thing over there worth a scrap is that pump and a horse trough that would make for a decent swimming hole.

So, I didn't ask Welby what happened, but it's hard keeping to your own business when there's so much of everybody else's business going on. Like Sharla's. She's my big sister and she's pregnant. I thought it was impossible for her and Toby to make a baby. He's half-bear, I swear it. He spits when he talks and his hands are covered in hair and you can hear his truck coming from a mile down. Sharla says she's not quitting school, but I wish she would. Everyone's talking about her.

I'm going to be an aunt, though, and I've never been a aunt or had an aunt so I don't really know what aunts do, but I'll be a good one I'm sure. After all, I had a chicken that I raised by myself. She wore a diaper. I'd put her in my bicycle basket and ride her down the road to my friend Maggie's, and she could go in Maggie's house because she had on that diaper. She was a good chicken, but one day her legs quit working. Welby said it was because she was pecking at a dead possum, but I'm not so sure. There were a lot of dangers around our place for a chicken, like the broken glass in the burn pit and the busted wood chipper and the dark crawl space under our house. Even Pip wouldn't go under there.

Sharla worried about cottonmouths. I don't know why. I think people make too big a stink about snakes. They think more of themselves than the snakes do. It's like when people say that mosquitoes bite them because they have sweet blood. They really shouldn't be so vain. Vanity is a sin. I know that much from the vacation bible school I went to with Maggie last summer at the Church of Christ. I mean, I've never had a snake run after me, but I can't say the same about mosquitoes. They get me a lot, and it's not because I'm sweet. The only person who ever called me sweet was a teacher at that vacation bible school, and that was only because I told her about the bug in her hair.

Welby belched. He always smelled like sour beer and dirt.

We turned into the Buckalew's driveway and I nearly fell off the tractor because Welby got too close to their mailbox and had to cut it quick. It was a new mailbox, he said, so he wasn't prepared.

The Buckalew's had gone to work in the city, so only their devil dog came out to see us and this time he didn't smell like baby powder. He smelled like a cross between sardines and a spit can and rotten eggs. I knew that smell. He had been sprayed by a skunk.

One whole side of the Buckalew's yard, between the driveway and their neighbor's pasture, was full of brambles and tires and whatnots. It was a low, wet spot. The neighbor's pond dumped into it, and not accidentally, which is why it was so wet and low. We got a spot like that at our place too. We just never cleaned it up.

Welby says the only reason people move out here is because they got nowhere to go or something to hide. The house had been empty for a year before the Buckalews bought it. A city cop from Memphis built it. He had lots of parties. Shot his own horse by accident. It jumped a fence and ended up down the road in Nettle's garden. She was hot mad but didn't act it because he was a cop. I think he had something to hide and she had no where to go.

He had a plane and a boat and a tractor too. I know cops in our town don't make that kind of money. Officer Josh, who works at our school, lives in a small house on Marginal Street with a pet parrot he confiscated, some hobby rockets, and a riding lawnmower. I think that's about all he has to his name, and I only know that because he tried to date Sharla.

One day that cop's big house went empty and before long the weeds had grown above my head. They grew so high that Maggie and I used her metal detector to search for pocket knives or buried money, but all we ever found was a busted-up beeper and a handful of nails and scrap. I took it all home to Welby. He didn't say so, but I knew he appreciated them.

The neighbor shot a bobcat in those weeds. Then he stuffed it and put it in front of his fireplace. After that, we didn't play there much.

Welby got right to work digging a hole with his backhoe and pushing the tires and brambles into it. Whenever he had a job, it usually meant him digging a hole, pushing stuff in it and setting it on fire. I sat at a safe distance in the culvert on the other side of the driveway thinking how we weren't so different, us and the Buckalews. They had nicer grass, sure, but we had the same clumps of buttercups and scraggly elms and wild honeysuckle and spiders in our ditches.

Soon after I sat down, I felt breath on my neck and I knew it was that devil dog. I could feel him staring straight at the back of my head, like he wanted to eat it, like I were some kind of roast. So, I crouched down and turned around real slow. I knew from TV that whenever you encounter a wild animal you don't make any sudden movements and you try to make yourself small. When I did, he licked my nose.

His name was Pepper Jack, according to his bright red tag. I think he knew I could help him. I had gotten skunk off dog twice before, after all, and it was time to do something productive. I grabbed a piece of hay string that was sticking out from under a rock in the ditch, tied it around the loop in his collar, and together we climbed out of the ditch.

I told Welby I was going back home, but I don't think he heard me. He was pouring diesel on the tires. Then, he lit a match and tossed it in. We watched them light up like our old Christmas tree, but they smelled awful. I swear the black smoke brought down at least one bluebird that didn't know any better to stay out of the way. I did.

Welby's shirt flapped in the wind. Sometimes he had trouble standing.

I looked from the tires to the dog to the road, and that's when I decided to take Pepper Jack home. He came without a fuss, which was a surprise to me. Pip would have never let me put a hay string on him.

Walking with a dog like Pepper Jack made me feel rich. Everything I had ever gotten in my life had been handed down or dug up or rescued. Nothing, not my dogs or my clothes or even my toys had ever been new. And I felt sorry, all of the sudden, for people who had to settle for ugly dogs. That's probably why momma left—to have nice dogs and better grass and new things.

Nettle yelled at me when I passed by, told me to put the wolf back where I got it. I put her in her place.

"It's not a wolf. It's a Siberian husky," I yelled.

"Well, it's gonna get shot, whatever it is," Nettle said, turning up her nose. "Someone's gonna think it's a wolf."

"I'm gonna wash him so he smells like baby powder. No wolf smells like baby powder. Everybody knows that."

She didn't have anything to say to that, as I expected. I picked a dandelion from her yard, stuck it in Pepper Jack's collar and moved on.

The Washingtons wouldn't take their eyes of him when we passed, like I was going to turn him loose to eat their dominos or their heads. I don't know why they were always so suspicious. If any of them had known what I was doing, they'd be praising me for my good deed, washing skunk off a stranger's dog. But they didn't ask. Adults don't ever ask the obvious questions. They just assume you're always up to something or out to get them. Or maybe they just wanted Pepper Jack for themselves and were waiting for me to let down my guard so they could take him.

I walked a little quicker.

Pip wasn't too happy with me bringing a new dog home. He snarled and dug into the dirt. Looked like a foaming rat. Pepper Jack just sat there and panted and looked around my yard like he had seen it before and couldn't care less about it the second time. I understood. He was probably used to his mowed grass and daffodil flowers, but I'm not convinced dogs care too much about fancy things. I tried to stuff Pip in a purse one time, like they do in Hollywood, and he nearly bit my finger off.

I tied Pepper Jack to the spigot, went and got the baking soda from the pantry and spilled over a jar of pickles doing it. The whole house smelled like pickle juice and garlic, but I didn't have time to clean it up. Pip was carrying on outside and making me nervous, so I had to get to it.

I got the dish detergent, ran down the hall and grabbed the peroxide from the bathroom. I mixed all the ingredients up in a bucket, took a rag and slopped it all over Pepper Jack. He was a good and patient dog. I think he knew what I was meaning to do.

You're supposed to leave the mixture on for a while before you rinse, so I flipped over the bucket and sat down, and I let him know it wouldn't be too long before he smelled like baby powder again. That didn't apply to his breath, though. There was nothing I could do about it aside from give him a good stick, but he wasn't interested in chewing.

I told him about my sister and her boyfriend and the moth that flew out of my ear. And he listened to me, not like Pip. You couldn't tell Pip anything for any period of time before he'd get sidetracked. I was thinking that maybe I should keep Pepper Jack because he was a good listener. Welby would understand. He'd be proud of me for taking what I wanted. And that's just what I was thinking about doing when the fire trucks began zooming by, blaring their sirens to let everyone know they were coming and to get out of their way. They came from all different directions, so long as they were left and right. Out where we live, there are only volunteer firefighters and no hydrants. So, they come from home, carrying yellow tanks of water on their trucks.

Then, Pepper Jack started howling like he was some kind of siren, too, and Pip, I couldn't believe it, joined in. I had never heard Pip howl. I was proud of him being so bold. So, I howled too, just to see what it was like, but Pepper Jack wasn't having any of it. He pulled and jerked and snarled until his tie snapped off the spigot, and I fell backwards trying to hold him back as he took off.

"Come back!" I yelled. "I haven't rinsed you off yet!"

But if he heard me he didn't act it, and soon all I could see was his white tail bobbing through Mr. Wilson's wheat field. Pip followed right behind. So I did what I had to do and ran off too.

I had to cross through two sets of barbed wire fences, a rutty cow pasture, somebody's bean field and a gulley before I came up into the Buckalews backyard. That's when I noticed the smoke.

The dogs had beat me there, of course, and were all in a tizzy. I don't think Pip had ever run that far, and Pepper Jack was near dry.

I looked around. I swear that fire skipped right over the Buckalew's fence, where Welby had started it, and hopped on over to the neighbor's pasture.

The fire trucks were parked in the pasture, and people had pulled over on the side of the road to watch. I don't know what entertained them more, one fireman's trying to get his hose untangled or Welby's getting good tongue lashing from Mrs. Buckalew, who had been called out of work.

"Are you drunk?" she yelled.

"No ma'm," Welby said, looking as fed up as I'd ever seen him.

"Then what the hell's wrong with you?"

(I don't think she saw me there. If she had seen me there she probably wouldn't have cursed. My momma cursed, but I didn't think rich people did. I thought they had better manners and all.)

"I'd rather discuss this with your husband," Welby said.

"My husband's an hour away. I'm here now and I'm telling you, we didn't hire you! We hired Josh."

Welby reached for his Hawkins chew, which is what he always did whenever someone brought up Josh. Josh was a Jenkins boy. The Jenkins had been in this town ever since horses hauled cotton. There's a sign dedicated to Josh's great grandaddy's honor in the town square.

"Josh is a Jenkins, you know," he said.

"What's wrong with the Jenkins'?"

"They cut corners."

Mrs. Buckalew threw up her hands and clunked in her heels over to a fireman. She was pretty but unprepared. She should know not to wear clothes like that in the country, skirts and high heels and such. You never know when you might need to stomp out a fire or wash skunk off a dog or hop on a tractor. But her gold jewelry sure did shine.

I'm not sure why she was so upset, though. It wasn't even her pasture that caught fire.

The firemen worked hard to put it out, but because it was a horse pasture, the manure kept flaming up, so I got out there and started stomping on it to help. But, I swear, as soon as I got one out, another would flame up, like those trick birthday candles. I spent the next two hours stomping out flames, long after Welby had left. Even Pip had gone and that was all right. I never let someone's leaving keep me from being productive. I didn't want the Buckalews to think poorly of us, and I didn't have anything else to do. Good thing I wore my boots. They were my mom's brown Durangos. They were her favorites, but the silver rings on the sides had started to rust and Pip had chewed around the top of the left boot.

The neighbors watched from the fence line, playing country music like it was a bonfire or something. They didn't seem worried—said the fire was good for their Bermuda but that I could keep stomping out the flames anyway because I was fun to watch.

The next day, Welby had me put a bill of services in the Buckalew's mailbox. He wrote something on it I can't repeat, but I scratched through it. I have a hunch he's not going to get paid. And Pepper, well, he's a bit lighter than he used to be. The peroxide bleached- his hair just like it had done Sharla's last summer. I'm sure he smells better, but I still smell like pickles.

The White Box

Everyone had warned it was going to be a hard winter because it had been a hard summer. First droughts, then floods. I hadn't even caught a fish until they spilled from the Loosahatchie into the parking lot of Kay's Food Mart. Floating ants were reported in Boondock's Ranch Supply, and a water moccasin was killed inside the bathroom of the filling station.

And then snow.

Maybe it wasn't so great for the farmers, but for me and Charlotte it was a miracle. (Daddy tells me not to use that word out of context with Jesus' workings, but anytime there's snow around Christmas in the South, it's a miracle, no matter what the Bible says.)

Charlotte and I plodded up a hill under the soggy sugar maples and pines. The sky was dull, but the air was sharp with cold and quiet—an occasional crackling of a broken limb, the distant squall of an anonymous bird.

My feet slipped and boots sank in the snow, making like the tracks of big wounded dogs. My boots were all wrong, a pair of leather-soled cowboy boots from the Trash to Treasure. They had no grip. And they were boy's boots, not that you could tell the difference. At least, I hoped you couldn't.

"So what'd you get for Christmas?" Charlotte asked.

I looked down at my boots.

"Oh," she brushed her bangs away, "is that all?"

"I got a rubber watch and a mood ring, too."

She looked at me for more, so I lied and added a clock radio.

"Cool. I got a tv," she said, smiling crooked.

She was lying too.

"Here, I got you something."

She pulled from her pocket a gold, broken heart attached to a small, yellow chain. It was the BFF necklace I had seen at the Dollar General, the kind where you wear half the broken heart and your best friend wears the other, and they're only whole when put together. I liked the idea of that.

She had taken a marker to the back and wrote our names on each of the pieces.

"I couldn't fit your whole name on the back, so I just put Anna. Who named you anyway?"

"My mom."

"Why'd she name you Annabelle? Kinda old-fashioned, don't you think?"

I wanted to ask Charlotte what it mattered what she named me, but she had just given me a necklace, and I liked that she was my friend. I didn't have many.

"It's a family name," I said, "my grandma's and great-grandma's."

My mom's name was Mabel. She was never happy about it, but that doesn't really matter now. What matters is I have Charlotte because when I said I didn't have many friends, I meant I only had one.

I toted the sled. My knit cap felt heavy and wet from the falling snow. Everything seemed still and unreal, like the settling of a snow globe or the strange silence of a funeral.

The light outside was dull and flat. It made the ground look the same everywhere, but the hill was good for sledding, as far as we could tell. The snow was thick, like the gator mud we'd play in after summer rains.

Half way up, as we stopped to check our surface and analyze a set of animal tracks, which we decided were rabbit, a snowball careened around a pine and splattered right in my face.

It was Charlie, and as usual, Judith was close behind.

Charlotte squealed, "Anna, you look like one of Jerry's snow cones!"

We'd go to Jerry's Snow Cones in the summer—shaved ice and ice cream mixed with flavoring. I always chose the wedding cake. Charlotte would pick grape and sour apple.

She laughed and brushed a line of snow off my forehead.

"Tastes like sugar."

She licked it off her mittens.

"Hey Charlie, come and have a bite!"

"I'd rather roll in pig shit," he said, and spat out a cigarette.

Charlie. He was named after his father. He always pretended he didn't like me, but I knew he did.

Suddenly, it felt hard to breathe.

"Pig shit!" Judith hollered from behind her brother.

She was only six. She shouldn't have been talking like that. What was worse was that she was always tailing Charlie. Wherever he went, there she was behind him poking fun at me.

"Go away, you little rat," Charlotte scolded and made rat-like noises.

Judith poked out her tongue and goggled her eyes. It looked like she was having some sort of fit.

"Why does she act like that?" I asked.

"She's jealous," Charlotte answered.

Charlie lit another cigarette and disappeared over the hill. I wanted to follow him, but I didn't.

"I am not jealous!" the little rat squealed.

"Are to!" Charlotte yelled.

"Am not!"

But Charlotte dug in and finished her off with a stare.

"Charlie! Charlotte says I'm jealous!" Judith looked around. "Charlie?"

She huffed through the snow and followed his tracks until she was gone too and I could breathe again.

"What's she so jealous of?"

Judith didn't know about the day I had spent with Charlie in the old copper stills last summer. No one knew. It was the only day we had ever spent together, so she couldn't have been jealous of me. No one was jealous of me.

"I'm prettier than she is," Charlotte said. "That's why she's jealous. And I have this, remember?"

She held up a charm bracelet with a chipped enamel unicorn, a silver scotty dog, and a locket. Inside the locket was a photo she had found in the abandoned Woodburn Plantation outside of town. It once was a halfway house for veterans. Now, it was nothing but a run-down old building that we dared each other to go in. And when we were brave enough, we found all sorts of things in there, like banged-up helmets the color of old spinach, flattened dog tags, carvings of naked girls and cartoons of generals in the busted up walls, and of course, the photo Charlotte kept in her locket of the young man she swore she knew in another life.

My dad would say that was sacrilegious.

She said the soldier's name was Billy. I said she was crazy. She said she hoped so.

"I think it'd be cool to be crazy, like living in a daydream."

She wouldn't say that to me now. Not to my face anyway.

But Charlotte had a strange take on things. Like this one time last summer, we watched Charlie working in the field. He was always working, and his father was always behind him surveying him and prodding at him, like he was a mule.

"Boy, you can do better'n that," he jabbed Charlie's side with walking stick.

His eyes were blue and bloodshot. His voice was hoarse with morning whiskey.

"Or are you a horsie's ass?"

"I ain't a horse's ass," Charlie mumbled.

"You are, aren't you? You're a horsie's ass," he teased.

Charlotte looked at me and smiled, a wheat stick in her mouth. I didn't see what there was to smile about. Her father was mean, but she was ok with that because he wasn't mean to her. She was his favorite.

"My father wouldn't tolerate that cursing," I told her.

"My daddy's not religious like yours."

She lifted her boot and read an inscription on the bottom.

"The eyes of the Lord are everywhere, keeping watch on the wicked and the good."

"That's a proverb," I said.

"Whatever it is, it shouldn't be on the bottom of my shoe."

I told my dad that once. I told him that people squash bugs and clean coops and skid down gravel and all kinds of things without thinking of their shoes, but he said he knew that. He said he was doing his part. He couldn't help if people weren't doing theirs by walking in the path of the Lord.

By passion, my father was a deacon at Faith Baptist and by profession a shoe mender. He repaired soles and pardoned no puns. That was his slogan. To him, they went hand-in-hand, or foot-in-foot, so he believed he was making all the right gestures required of faithful servants by carving Bible passages in the soles of his customers' shoes.

"What does it say on the bottom of your boots?" she asked, as I slipped in the snow.

"Nothing."

"Really? You mean your daddy put nothing on the bottom of those shiny boots you got for Christmas?"

"Maybe they were from Santa."

"Santa? Come on!"

I couldn't tell her no for long. She had the bluest eyes. I couldn't ever look away from them. And she was my best friend. She told me often. I liked that she would tell me so often. And now I had a necklace to prove it.

So I showed her my sole, and she read it.

"The path of life leads upward for the wise to keep him from going down to the grave."

She frowned.

"That's sad," she said.

I shrugged.

"No one sees the bottom anyways."

But I hated it. I hated that he put that on my boots. He could've picked any other of the thousands of verses, but he chose that one.

Charlotte stopped and turned to me.

"I'm sorry about your mom," she said.

I tried to respond but my throat was like cotton.

"I never told you, but I was always sorry."

I didn't know what to say. I was tired of hearing how sorry people were anyway.

"Why do you think she did it?" she asked.

And I wanted to yell, *Why bother wondering why?* I wanted to scream it. It was something I would never understand. It was a stupid question. I was only sure of one thing.

"She was unhappy," I said, and continued walking.

It was the first time I had said it out loud. I don't know why she was unhappy. Maybe it was her name. Maybe it was me. My father thought she needed mending, like an old shoe, but he was never able to fix her. So he resigned the task to God and apologized for it in about the same way a neighbor apologizes for tall grass.

"Want me to carry the sled?" Charlotte asked as I passed her.

I shook my head. We walked some distance in silence. It was getting colder.

"Do you believe in heaven?" she asked.

It was a stupid question because if I didn't believe in heaven, then my mom was just another body in a white box—a white pine box with brass handles. That was what she asked for in the letter she left. That kind of box wasn't easy to find. You'd think it would be. But we had to have it made five counties over. The carpenter was fat and shiny. I didn't like him, but he made a nice box.

"When my dad shot Smokey 'cause he went lame, he said he went to heaven. I think he said that just to make me feel better."

"Smokey was just a horse, Charlotte."

"Well, if I went lame I wouldn't want anyone putting a bullet in my head. And if there are no horses in heaven, then I don't wanna go."

Charlotte was Catholic. If she was Baptist like me, she wouldn't question these things, but sometimes I felt that my faith put me at a disadvantage. There was only one God, but there were seven devils for each of the deadly sins. When you're outnumbered like that, it's easy for a devil to sidetrack you and tempt you with all sorts of sinful things. That's what my dad said happened to my mom. She got sidetracked.

The hike up the hill started to take some effort.

"Where do you think Charlie went?" I asked.

"Probably over to Tammy's. He says she puts out."

Clearly he didn't say the same of me. I don't think Charlotte would still be my BFF if she knew I had spent the entire summer dreading the baby that I was certain was forming inside me after I met Charlie in the stills. Turns out, kissing doesn't get you pregnant.

The stills were up on Pokey Moonshine Road shacked up in an old barn.

Charlie and I met there last summer, and we sat on a blanket that smelled like moldy hay. He said he had never brought another girl to the stills, and I believed him because it was summer. And I was in love.

"I love you," I told him, before I knew to be afraid to say that to boys.

He kissed me, so I assumed I had said the right thing until he said, "You don't know what love is."

That bothered me, but he was, after all, four years older than me and knew more about these things.

So I asked, "Then what is it, Charlie?"

I could hear him breathing, and I wished I could breathe that easily. I always felt like I was holding my breath, and then I'd forget that I was holding it and I'd have to let it out all at once before I turned a color.

He looked around the barn for something to help answer the question. It was cluttered with the scraps of bubblegum wrappers, bird feathers, yellowed newspapers, car parts. His set his eyes on a round, busted headlight.

"It's like when a car's side by side of yours, and it begins to speed up. Without thinking you speed up too and start goin' really fast before you realize it. That's how love is."

"Sounds like fun."

"Yeah, then you slow down."

My mom once told me that love is all those things you can't hold in your hands but you can feel. But in my hands at that moment was Charlie's thigh. That was real and warm. I could feel him, his blue jeans, grass-stained and patched over. I pulled his leg closer to me, lifted it, and placed it over my own.

No matter how I placed my mother's hands, there was no life to them, no warmth. They just lay there in that white box.

What did she know about love anyway? She wasn't there. All she could ever do is sing.

This little light of mine, I'm gonna let it shine.
This little light of mine, I'm gonna let it shine.
Let it shine, let it shine, let it shine.
Won't let Satan blow it out, I'm gonna let it shine.
Won't let Satan blow it out, I'm gonna -

"Hurry up slowpoke!" Charlotte called from the top of the hill.

I don't know when she passed me.

We looked down the hill together. It was a wide-open run, straight and steep with a dip in the middle like a chunk was carved out with a pocketknife.

I wondered if her heart was racing like mine.

I looked back and traced our tracks from where we had begun at the edge of the road. There was a creek that ran alongside it. Cattails sprouted there thick in the summer and crabapples bobbed from knobby trees, but the creek was nearly frozen now.

If we got up enough speed, our run would direct us straight for the road, over the dip and through the creek, and then between two trees in the field on the other side. The field still had corn stubs in it, sticking out of the snow like buried crosses, and the two trees stood on the edge of it. They were big and old. The branches of one tree reached up. The branches of the other tree bent down.

My mom once told me that they were reaching for each other. She said that under the ground their roots tangled and twisted into one, even though they couldn't touch above the earth.

Not long after that, one of the trees caught a worm and died.

Charlotte secured the sled. The sun was breaking through, sparkling on the snow. It reminded me of the runway at the city airport with bits of glass in it.

The snow had stopped falling, but flurries dusted the air like pigeon feathers.

Charlotte kissed the locket with the soldier's picture for luck and tucked it back into the sleeve of her yellow turtleneck. Her lips were pink and cheeks wind-burned.

"Why did you name him Billy?" I asked.

"I didn't name him. That's just his name."

"How do you know?"

Charlotte smiled.

"I just know, like you know the words in the Bible are real. His name is Billy."

She took her seat at the front of the sled. I took the back, the "knocker" position we called it because you got knocked around a lot.

"Ready?" she asked.

"Ready," I said.

We didn't make it to the trees or across the road or even to the frozen creek. We were thrown through the air midway down at the dip in the hill. And when we realized that we were both all right, we laughed and climbed the hill again.

The Lost Dog

I

It would've been a forgetful house if it hadn't been so close to the road, built right into the bend. No telling how many ordinances he broke building it there, but no one seemed to care except the rich man and he really only cared about himself.

Old Man Scrap won the lot from him betting on a horse. The rich man bet Scrap his horse would win Best of Show in the McNabb Cotton Arena. People from as far away as three counties came with their trailers and their fly sprays and their braided horses to compete in it. I don't know why the rich man bet him—because he could, I guess. He probably figured his money bought him smarts. That, and Scrap provoked him with a remark about his stallion's persuasion.

But the rich man lost. He had underestimated Scrap's spotted saddle horse. Sometimes a low stock can breed a high line, that's what my granddaddy used to say. It also helped that the rich man's horse lost a shoe in mid-canter, causing quite a fit in the ring. It was in the paper the next day, the rich man flailing through the air, projected from his glossy, red steed like a fat gnat flicked from a peach.

Fanning the fire was the horse. I swear it was laughing, at least his gums and all his teeth were showing.

Even the part where the rich man lost one-fourth of an acre and cried foul was in the Fayette Falcon, which is probably why he made good on his word. He was a businessman first, after all, and doing big business in a small town meant you had to keep your dealings up or your head low. He wasn't about keeping his head low, but since he didn't specify the plot he was going to surrender, he gave Scrap the worst one, filled with rock and sand and tires from old construction. It would've been nothing to the rich man, except to show that he had one more one-fourth of an acre, and except that Scrap built himself a new house right on top of it.

Guess the rich man didn't see that coming. One man's one-fourth of an acre is another man's ponderosa, I suppose. But what else did he think Scrap would do with it? Watch it grow over? That was the problem with the rich folks – what they gain in ease they lack in imagination.

Scrap had to cut into the land to build his little, brown house, so his back yard was flat for about ten steps and then butted up against a dirt wall. He kept a dog pen, a John boat and the saddle horse back there, tied up to a gum tree, along with a weight bench, some tiki torches and a rusty smoker.

He knew that the rich man gave him poor soil but he didn't care. He used the horse as both lawn mower and fertilizer. It would be fertile ground in a year or two, he said, after which he would grow a small tomato garden. Every morning for breakfast he ate a tomato and mayonnaise sandwich with salt and pepper. Having grown up in Ripley, he hated buying tomatoes that weren't grown from some farmer he knew firsthand. It was unnatural. So he raked and spread Rusty's fresh manure himself every morning and threw anything back there he didn't eat, creating one big compost pile like some kind of accidental ecosystem.

There was a clump of irises on the edge of the property, straddling the barbwire fence that the rich man put in after he gave it away. They were as big as me and nearly overtook with weeds. I wanted to divide them up. I knew how to divide things up—dress hems, daylilies, Momma and Daddy. Mrs. Early, our neighbor, has irises and amaryllis flowers everywhere. They take to our clay like weeds. She said God put them here for us as a testament to his love, and for the birds and bugs, but that people didn't appreciate them. She said they'd just as well kill everything off, every little dandelion and buttercup to seed a patch of Bermuda like they were covering a stain on the floor with a rug.

If you ask me, one kind of everything means all kinds of nothing. I think that's why Daddy was always in trouble. He didn't want to be a nothing. I think if he had spent more time admiring the weeds in his own backyard and all the bees and butterflies that lived off them, he would've appreciated his own standing more. But they probably would have just reminded him of all those things he thought he hadn't accomplished. For some, a weed can make you feel that way.

I hung around Scrap because I could. Momma was always working and Daddy was jailed. Scrap used to tell me to get on. He said I was like a ladybug, clinging to windows as soon as it warmed up, and once you started swatting at one, another would just show up.

I'd sit at his card table, stacking his dominoes, watching his T.V. He always watched *Wheel of Fortune* real loud. I never liked puzzles, but I liked to see what Vanna was wearing. She always wore the dresses you could only find at the mall or in magazines, or, if you were lucky, hand-me-downed at the thrift shop. One day I just knew I'd create dresses like that. In the mean time, I made my own with scraps Momma would pick up for me at thrift stores and garage sales. She had an old Singer from the 70's. It looked like it had been sitting in the deep end of a pool for years, like it was some kind of space trash that fell from the sky and landed there. It weighed a ton, but it worked. I made my own curtains out of old nightgowns and Barbie clothes. I'm thinking of entering them in the fair.

Anyway, Scrap was real good at solving those word puzzles.

"Amos Moses Was a Cajun" he would yell or "Take the Money and Run". I don't know how he did it, filling in the letters like that, but he almost always got them right, and he didn't even go to college. I bet he'd beat that rich man. I'm sure of it. The only thing that rich man was better at than Scrap was talking other folks out of their money. In the Bible it says that where your treasure is so is your heart. Scrap's heart was in a different place is all, although to where and which I couldn't say.

He was three letters up and two down when the phone rang. I think it had once been white, that phone, but now it was a brownish-gray, like the color of old milk. He had it on speaker cause he was hard of hearing, so I heard every call he got and most I shouldn't. Sometimes I think he forgot I was even there.

"Barry?" the man on the line asked.

He had a high voice that made me nervous. If you're at peace with life, you don't have a high voice. You have a smooth and soft voice like Dean Martin, my momma's favorite singer.

Scrap stuffed his lip with chew.

"No, this ain't Barry," he replied.

"This ain't Barry White?"

"No."

"I must'a got the wrong number."

"Barry's my dog. You know, like the singer."

"What singer?"

"Barry White, the Love Doctor."

"I don't know no Love Doctor, Mister."

"I ain't no Mister. I'm Scrap."

"Scrap?"

"Scrap Cannon."

"Oh, I thought your dog was Scrap."

"I'm Scrap. He's Barry. What's this about?"

"It's about your dog. I got your dog."

"Well, I figured someone did," he said and spit into a coffee can.

I didn't even realize Barry was missing. He was a sheep of a dog, skittish and tuck-tailed. He hardly ever made a sound. Scrap swore by his instincts as a hunter though.

"You lose him at the lodge?" the man asked.

"Yep, last week."

Scrap talked out of the corner of his mouth. I don't know how he did it, how the words came out, but they did. He had palsy that made his face twist up. Between that and his chew, there was a constant run of brown spit down his chin. After a while you didn't notice it. Sometimes I wondered if he did it on purpose just to keep people from bothering him. I wouldn't put it past him.

"You comin' back soon?" the man asked.

"I was only comin' if someone fount my dog. They up'd the dues, so I won't be huntin' there no more."

"Yeah. I suppose they've got to, improvements and all."

Scrap grunted. He was suspicious of any change labeled as improvement or improvement labeled as progress.

"He's a good lookin' hound, ain't he?" Scrap prodded.

"Uh, he's alright, I guess."

"Alright? He's from the Prince Albert Piney line. Finest blood in Mississippi and, I'd challenge, Louisiana."

"Well, I'm gonna leave him tied to the hitching post. When are you comin' up?"

"I'll be up this evenin', I reckon. Who is this?"

"Randy Mack, Porter's nephew."

"A'right, Randy. Thanks for findin' my dog."

"Well, I wasn't lookin' for him so I don't reckon I found him, but you're welcome just the same."

II

I had to beg Scrap to let me go with him. Well, that's not entirely true. I asked and he grunted and I got in his truck, but I felt real pushy about it. He's got a way of making you feel like you're in the wrong place asking the wrong questions at the wrong time. But I didn't have anywhere to be with school out on break and all. Momma wouldn't be home until late and even then she wouldn't notice me gone until the next morning when her breakfast wasn't ready. It's not her fault. She's just always tired from working. I think she worries more than her body can keep up with. I never mind cooking breakfast. It makes me feel responsible for something, but I'm about tired of grits and powdered eggs. I think I'll get us some chickens. I've seen other people with chickens. All you've got to do is put them in the yard and they eat bugs and lay eggs for you. Nothing comes as easy as that. Except one time Mrs. Early gave us a dozen eggs to help us through one of Daddy's goings-away. I boiled them for egg salad and when I went to shell them there were baby chicks inside. They came out like an unset Jell-O mold. It was awful. Momma said to never accept eggs from Mrs. Early again no matter how well-meaning she was about it.

The lodge was a couple hours away, past Selmer down 64 and through the Hatchie River bottoms. Then, it was one winding back road after another until we came up to a cabin through a stretch of pines. I've never been farther than Hardeman county, and that was to visit Daddy, but one day I'll go to New York City where the skyscrapers go on as far as our pines. I'll be fortunate to have seen both versions of heaven, one made by man and one by God.

The cabin was called Chickasaw Lodge, by way of the sign hanging over it with two tomahawks crossed like a coat of arms. The front porch had 13 sets of deer antlers and one hog's head nailed to the wall. A stuffed beaver was screwed on the railing and a stuffed possum over the door, open-mouthed and snarly like it dared you to come in.

Scrap got out of the truck. It was an old Ford truck, red and white and heavy metal and the doors made themselves known when they shut, hushing up the frogs and cicadas for a good minute. A man walked out from the cabin. Some would call him handsome, but I wouldn't. I don't call any man anything other than a man. Men are men and women are women and that's all there is to it. The only variations that exist in us other than our body parts are the types of graces other folks expect of us. Anyway, this particular man was wearing camouflage overalls and a white t-shirt. He didn't have on shoes, just dirty white socks and one with a hole that his big toe fit through like a fish through a net. I wanted to sew it up for him. No one should have holey socks. You could get a needle and thread at the Dollar General for $1.29 and it takes nothing to sit for a minute and mend.

He held a mason jar half full of shine. By the way he swayed, as if the floor were crooked or wind was hard, I assumed the jar had once been full. For some reason, I wanted to feed him, like a stray dog, like he needed taking care of.

Scrap leaned on the hitching post and I looked around for another one because I remembered that the man on the phone said Barry was tied to the post. There was the post and, sure enough, there was a dog, but it wasn't Barry.

"You Randy?" Scrap asked.

"Yeah, you Scrap?"

He nodded.

"You look like your uncle," said Scrap.

Randy smiled slow and crooked.

"People say he's a handsome man. I'll take that as a compliment."

His words rolled into one. His voice sounded deeper

and slower than on the phone like he was talking from under his own foot.

"So where's my dog at, Randy?"

Randy looked both ways down the road as if he'd practiced the gesture. Then he did it again. Measure twice, cut once, Granddaddy would say.

"He was here, I swear it," Randy said.

"You said he was tied up to this post. Only dog out here is this sorry lookin' Juniper."

Randy leaned in as if he hadn't seen it before.

"This is Willis' dog," Scrap said slowly to be sure he was heard correctly. "She's been lost for near a month."

"Well, I'll be. Willis was here today and I saw him pick up a dog. I just figured he had got this one. It came up later."

It was dark, but I could tell Scrap was red-faced and holding in his breath by how his shoulders raised up. I thought I might do better to get back in the truck. I'd seen him like this once before when the police came to his house with a citation for littering for the trash that blew out of his truck, like he could help it.

"Where is Willis now?" he asked as slowly as I'd ever heard him speak, almost like he couldn't get the words out. "And why'd he take my dog?"

Randy shifted his feet and looked behind him as if for some kind of reinforcement.

"I don't know," he shrugged, "but can you blame him? I've heard Juniper ain't worth a damn."

"You can't go and steal another man's dog just 'cause your own ain't worth a damn!"

Randy took a swig and smiled.

"Folks do it all the time with their wives."

"Wives ain't worth a damn neither. I've had three. When they get to yappin' I just drive 'em down the road a ways and let 'em out. Ain't had one come back since."

"Here's to that," Randy raised his glass to the moon.

I couldn't tell if he was keeping his drink steady or it was keeping him. One was the aider and one the abettor. All I knew is that I wouldn't ever be anyone's wife.

"If Willis stole my dog, then I'll just steal his," Scrap decided.

"You don't wanna to do that. He's sore with ticks."

"Just help me get 'em in the back, Randy."

"I ain't touchin' that dog. And I ain't aidin' a thief."

"By God, you aided Willis. You're gonna aid me."

"I did not aid Willis," he said like it was the truest statement he had ever made.

"Then how'd you know he took my dog?"

"I saw him out the window, but I didn't help him."

"That makes you a witness and I need a witness. You're coming with us too."

"No I ain't!"

"Yes, you are!"

And when Scrap says you're going do something, you're going to do it. He took Randy by the scruff and shoved him in the cab of the truck where he sat looking long and sorry, especially after Scrap poured out his drink. Scrap hadn't touched a drop in 40 years. He said liquor was the devil's water and you can tell it by the fire that it makes going down.

I got in one side of the truck and Scrap got in the other, so Randy was stuck solid in between.

"We're goin' to see Willis," Scrap said, after putting the dog in the back, and that was that.

Randy looked at me like he couldn't figure out where I had come from. He smelled like rotgut and onions and that hole in his sock bothered me like an itch, so I just turned my head and cracked the window.

Scrap peeled away from the lodge, scattering gravel and flinging poor Juniper across the back. Randy bobbed up and down on the bench seat like a cork. We were almost clear of the pines and to the highway when all of the sudden a deer flew out of the woods like it had been projected by a fairy cannon, and I wouldn't have believed it didn't have wings if I hadn't seen it dead one minute later. It slammed into Scrap's grill, rolled up and over the hood and the windshield, and landed right in the bed of the truck like that's exactly where it had intended to be. It was deader than dead. The only deer I had ever seen more dead than that one was the one that Daddy came home with after a week of hunting in the Arkansas bottoms. It looked like it had been scooped up from the side of the road, and now I'm sure it had been after seeing this one, especially since, at that time, it was hog season.

We sat there in the cab of the truck for a minute, stunned and silent, Scrap gripping the steering wheel, Randy swaying like the truck had never stopped, and me searching the woods for any members of the deer's immediate family. Scrap turned and peered through the dusty back window to make sure that Juniper was all right and the deer was still dead before he took a deep breath and moved on.

III

Ruby came out in a bright pink leotard and headband. She was barefoot and sweating. Her veins puffed up from her arms like ants tunneled through them, and her hair was an unnatural red. She looked like a half-cocked rooster.

"Scrap! Hell, it's you! I thought you was the postman."

"This late?"

"I was expecting something mail order off the TV. It boils eggs in the microwave. I had to have it."

She eyed Scrap like something else she might have to have.

"What are you doin' down here anyway? It aint't nothin' of a hop-skip from your place."

"Your husband stole my dog," he said.

He always got straight to the point.

"He did what?"

"Willis. He stole my dog."

"My husband? Stole? That don't sound like him."

"Well, he stole it, Ruby. I have it on good account."

He pointed to Randy in the truck, who, in my opinion, looked more like a no-account, but nobody asked me.

"Scrap, you're talking about Willis, the man that walked out of the Food Rite with a Coca-Cola he forgot to pay for and can hardly go in there now where he don't feel like he's being watched. I told him don't no one care about that damn Coca-Cola, but he swears they've got him on tape somewhere."

Scrap grunted and hitched up both legs of his britches like he was settling his feet for a siege.

"Then how come I got your dog in my truck?" he asked.

"Juniper?"

He nodded.

"Hell, I hate that dog. I thought she was gone for good. You can keep her."

"I don't want her, Ruby. I want my dog. Willis took my dog and left his"

"Your dog ain't here, Scrap, and I think I'd know."

Scrap looked into the darkness like Willis might've been hiding the dog in it. Where he could've hidden him I couldn't say. There wasn't anything there at the bottom of the hill where they lived but a metal glider swing, a bush hog, a burn barrel, and a ditch.

Scrap whistled, just to see what might come of it. Nothing did.

"See," she said and put her hand on her hip like it belonged there.

"I'll just wait for Willis," he said.

"Well, you might as well wait for him inside. I'm in the middle of my exercises but I don't mind a little company."

He followed her, after he first told me and Randy to stay put, but Randy's face was looking scowly. I think that stopping the truck gave his body time to catch up to what he had been putting inside of it and I didn't want to be there when it found its way back out. So, I snuck around the house and found an open window behind a sticky bush where I could keep watch on Scrap. He didn't know it, but I kept watch on him a lot. I did all kinds of things for him when he wasn't looking, like taking the boiled water off the stove and picking the weeds from his air conditioner. I'm sure once or twice I helped him avoid disaster, but I can't account for what happens when I'm not around. I guarantee it that if I had been at that lodge, Barry would've never gone missing.

Ruby led Scrap into the living room like some kind of realtor, like she was selling him on her ability to keep a tidy home. It had brown furniture, green curtains, brass glass tables and, in front of the TV, of all things, a mini-trampoline.

I would have put some appliqués on the curtains and trim around the lampshades, but that's just me.

"Take a seat in that recliner there," Ruby said, doing her best to round out her straight hips like the girls from The Pony nightclub. I'm not allowed in there but I know Daddy's been because a girl I went to school with saw him there. She dropped out and got a job as a singing waitress because the tips were good. Last I heard, she had dyed her hair white and was both singing and dancing.

Scrap sat in the recliner, but he sat straight up in it like his jeans were starched too heavy. I had never seen him look so uncomfortable.

"I got 25 minutes left on this tape and I ain't stoppin'. If I stop too long my legs go all wobbly. I made that mistake once and busted right through the wall and into the bathroom. Willis was hot mad. It'll be good to have someone to talk to. I ain't never got no one to talk to 'cept Celia and she's touched."

"No need to talk. I don't want no accidents."

"Oh, I'm a natural-born multi-tasker," she said, stepping on the trampoline. "You should'a seen me when I was barrel racin'. Willis used to look at me like I put every star in the sky. He don't look at me like that no more. I swear he looks at Juniper with more affection than me and your horse. That's a fine horse. I want a man to look at me like that again," she trounced. "You're a man. Would you look at me like that if I weren't married?"

Scrap sat up straighter.

"Can't say."

"Why not? I'm just askin'."

"It ain't a right thing to ask, Ruby."

"Oh, ain't no harm in it. See how healthy I am on this trampoline? I can go for days."

Scrap fidgeted in his seat like he had some kind of rash until he finally stood up and said he was leaving.

"Aw, just stay a while. I ain't gonna bite you. I can't promise I won't just fall into those big ole your arms of yours . . . on accident, you know," she winked.

"I ain't gonna catch you if you do."

"Now that ain't right," she whined.

"You ain't right, Ruby. I'm leavin'. Tell Willis that when I get my dog back, he can have his."

"You can't thieve 'cause you were thieved. It's in the Bible."

"So is whorin'."

"You son-of-a-bitch!" she hollered. "You callin' me a whore?"

Of course, Scrap calls them like he sees them. In my opinion, most people don't like hearing what they know to be true when it's not flattering, and even though she seemed like something of the come-along-easy type, she wasn't about to admit it. In fact, she was so hot about it she flew off that trampoline like it had scaled her toes. Her body turned into a projectile aimed directly at Scrap and landed smack on his back as he was turning to go. Fortunately for her, Scrap was a man of some upbringing, his father having served in two wars and he in one, so his natural inclination was to keep her from falling once she had landed. He grabbed onto her legs and rounded his back to hold her weight at the same time yelling at her to get off.

"I'll scratch your eyes out for callin' me a whore," she yelled.

He shook and turned circles but she clung to him like a wet cat to a stump in the middle of the river. He swung around with such a whirl that her foot flung loose and knocked a lamp off a table. The carpet was thick and padded its landing, which gave them both a moment of pause and Ruby an opportunity to change her attitude, as if he were suddenly her accomplice in a crime that never actually happened.

"I'm light, ain't I?" she wiggled and grinned.

"What?"

"You like me, don't ya?"

"I don't fool with married women!"

"But Willis ain't no good," she whined. "He tricked me into marryin' him. Said he had big plans. His plans weren't no bigger than his—"

And that's when Willis busted into the living room. He was as wide as Ruby was small, made like a Lego, like you could build a fort with him.

"Scrap Cannon!" he yelled. "What in the hell is my wife doin' on your back?"

Poor Scrap just stood there, his mouth wide open, the juice of his chew oozing down his chin. His arms hung limp at his side and even though he stood up straight and quick, Ruby still clung to him.

"I can sure tell you this, Willis. I didn't put her there," he said, trying to catch his breath.

"I thought I saw a spider, honey," Ruby lied, flapping her lashes.

Lucky for Scrap he had the benefit of a solid reputation. People could believe that the first time Scrap said something, it carried as much weight as the second and third, so he didn't do a lot of repeating.

"Woman! Get off that man's back!" Willis hollered.

"But I'm light as a feather. You see this?" she bounced. "I'm light as a feather."

"Get off him or so help me I'll-"

"You'll what?"

His fists balled up and cheeks went tight. His flat top stood up higher than it had when he came in, like a dog whose back hairs lift when it's angry. He stared at his wife like he had all kinds of words he was holding back, but it made his mouth full of nothing but air and no vocabulary.

"Just brush her off, Scrap," Willis finally mumbled.

"I ain't some chigger he can just brush off," she antagonized.

"You're right about that, Woman. You're like a tick you gotta take tweezers to."

"See! I tolt you he weren't no good, didn't I, Scrap?" she said, climbing down and huffing off to the bathroom.

Willis opened the fridge, took out some string cheese, and ate it like a carrot.

"I know you ain't come for my wife," he said, "So why are you here?"

"I came for my dog."

"Your dog?"

"Yeah, why'd you take my dog?"

"It was tied to a post. It weren't right to see such a fine dog tied to a post."

"Why didn't you take your own dog?"

"Juniper?"

"Yeah, Juniper."

"She's dead."

"She ain't dead. She's in the back of my truck."

"She's alive?" he jumped up.

I half expected the ground to shake when he landed.

"How's she look?"

"Sore with ticks."

"Hot damn, that's my Juniper!"

"So where's Barry?"

"I left him tied to the tree."

"You just said it weren't right to see such a fine dog tied up."

"There weren't no where else to put him at your house, you old fool."

"He's at my house?"

"Yeah, what do you take me for, a thief?"

"That's exactly what he takes you for, Willis," Ruby said.

"Hush, Woman!"

"Hush yourself! Now you both got your dogs back, go on about your business and get."

"This is my house," Willis stomped, his body stiff and impenetrable, like a retaining wall.

"This ain't a house," she flailed her arms around its space.

"It's a trailer and it ain't even a double wide. You said when we was married you'd get me a house."

"You don't like it, you can get!"

"See how he talks to me, Scrap? What'd I tell you? He ain't no good."

"Tell you what, Scrap, when you go you can take Ruby with you, but leave the dog."

"That's it!" she threw up her hands. "I'm gone for good, Willis! I ain't just sayin it this time. It's really happenin'. You see how he talks to me, Scrap? You see how he talks to me?"

I couldn't help but snicker. I saw an old black and white movie one time, one of those where the actors didn't talk. There was just music and words on the screen and so everything they did was exaggerated, I guess so you'd get the point faster. That's what she reminded me of, as if her body were too small to contain the emotions inside of it.

She disappeared into a back room. Willis offered Scrap a cheese stick. Scrap declined.

"Let's just get your dog," he said.

I ran back to the truck as fast as I'd ever run and tripped over my own feet getting in, falling into Randy like a loon. He looked at me again like he never seen me before and I had the strong urge to feed him some bologna and crackers. Scrap got Juniper out of the truck and handed him over. You would've thought he had raised the dog from the dead himself from the way Willis carried on over the both of them—Juniper for being alive and Scrap for resurrecting him.

I've never been attached to any animal. At my house, they come and they go all the time and not one of them ever stayed for longer than a week before they ran back off. I always figured they didn't take to me, and that was ok. I'm used to being on my own. You should never get too attached to things.

Scrap got back in the truck and started backing up, but Ruby ran out the front door and down the steps with a duffle bag in one hand and her trampoline in the other. She had on a bright pink sweatshirt with letters across it that spelled "Firecracker."

I'm not sure if she wore anything else.

"Drop me off at my momma's, Scrap," she said and threw her stuff in the bed of the truck.

She saw me and Randy in the front and smiled as if to indicate a kindness in exchange for a seat, but neither Randy nor I were budging. Then, she looked at me as if she belonged more rightfully in my place, but she was mistaken. So she huffed real loud and climbed up on the back tire before letting out a scream that could've brought coyotes running for a stuck rabbit.

"I ain't sitting back here with no roadkill!"

I think we had all forgotten about the deer, all but Juniper, anyway. She had been chewing on a leg the entire ride.

Scrap told her she would sit back there or stay where she was and he didn't care which. So, she crouched down in the farthest corner of the bed of the truck, next to the tailgate. Her momma lived only a quarter mile down the road anyway. She could've walked if she was that determined, but I supposed it wouldn't have been practical carrying a trampoline down a dark road at night. Either way, we got her there and that was that with Ruby.

IV

We had to drive all the way back to the lodge to drop off Randy. Seemed like a lot of work for nothing. He hadn't been much of a witness and on the way he got his second wind after we pulled over and let him vomit. That made him nothing if not very talkative and I didn't much care for his conversation.

"I don't believe it," Scrap said.

"I tell you, it happened," Randy asserted. "It happened just like I said and Shane's in jail now for animal cruelty. Stomped that puppy in front of his granny, right on her front porch."

"I'm trying to eat, Randy," I said.

We had all gotten hungry and stopped at Gurkins for snacks. Scrap's was a sack of fried chicken gizzards, Randy's was a bag of Twizzlers and mine was hot fries and chocolate milk. I wanted Randy to get something more substantive to eat, but he said he had a craving and who was I, his momma?

We rode in silence past little white houses glowing under electric poles, quick stops with beer and bait and lottery tickets, and church signs with Sunday service times and quotes that were supposed to inspire. I didn't go to church, but I heard a Mennonite sermon once on a CD they were giving away free at their bakery. In the sermon, the preacher said that as a child he was afraid of the Northern Lights because his father had told him that God was in the lights. He wouldn't look at them because he was afraid God would know his thoughts and that he was a sinner. But I would be ok with God knowing my thoughts and I love looking at Mrs. Early's irises. I wouldn't be afraid of anyone who created those. It's my Daddy I wouldn't want knowing my thoughts.

I leaned my head against the window and pulled my sleeves over my hands. I was suddenly very tired so I closed my eyes. My mind drifted to those weird random things that tend to go through my head before sleep, like the macaroni and cheese I would fix on the stove the next day and whether Ruby would go back to Willis and how the sound of truck tires on asphalt reminded me of an electric razor. But just as I was drifting off, Randy started up again.

"Anyway, after Shane stomped that puppy, he hid out in an abandoned house on Crump. He stole chickens from the Culver's for three weeks until they finally set up a game camera and caught him. So he was charged with both animal cruelty and animal theft. Lucky for Shane that when the Culver boys found him Pierre was with him. Pierre hates them Culver's and they fought it out in a mud hole until the police arrived. Police couldn't tell one from the other until they got a hose to them. Say, where you goin?"

Scrap had slowed down and turned off the highway towards an orange and green neon sign that blinked, *Jack's Deer Processing*. It lit up the sky above the trees like the star of Bethlehem.

Scrap parked underneath it.

"Help me get that deer out," he told Randy.

After Randy relieved himself behind the truck, not even warning me not to look, they dragged the deer to the front porch. I followed. It sure was a sorry prize. Five other much finer looking, cleaner kills hung on hooks in various stages of dressing—one with no back strap, another with no skin, and another missing legs. They all had racks, from twelve to four. A pile of hides lay in the corner, discarded like folds of dirty laundry. It smelled like metal, decay and pepper, just as I had remembered.

All that separated the front porch from the shop was a broken screen door and Jack, who sat behind a metal desk in a swivel chair that molded around his body like he'd been born into it. The leather was faded and duck taped in parts and it blatted like an old, rubber squeeze toy with the slightest movement of his body.

"Ain't you Drasco's young'un?" Jack asked me.

I nodded.

"Shame what happened to him, just a shame."

He looked at me, expecting a comment, like they always did, so I just agreed, like I always had.

"What's your name again?"

"Maxleigh."

"Pick you out a track over there, Maxleigh," he said, pointing with a pen to a box of 8-track cassettes.

People offer you the strangest things when they feel sorry for you. That's why I liked being with Scrap. He never offered me anything, so I didn't feel obliged to always say thank you for things I didn't want.

I walked over to the cassettes. I only knew what they were because of an old car Daddy once had, but I didn't recognize any of the names. I just picked the one that looked the cleanest.

"John Denver," Jack smiled. "That's a good'un. Put it in."

Jack asked Scrap what he got and Scrap showed him. Didn't bother Jack any what the carcass looked like. I'm sure he'd seen so many he wasn't surprised anymore by what people brought him. It would be like being a preacher and listening to people confess their sins day in and day out. You'd get used to it. After a while, they probably wouldn't sound so bad because you'd gotten used to them and then one day you'd just start sinning yourself since everyone else was already doing it anyway.

"You want sausage?" Jack asked Scrap.

"And ham steak, stew meat and butterfly loins," he replied.

"I'll get you what I can but I can't tell how bad she is until I get in her."

Scrap nodded.

"What about jerky? Try my jerky, you'll love it."

He talked like his tongue was too big for his mouth and his body too big for his skin. His hands were thick and rough and stained with blood and spice. His belly poked out over his jeans and through his leather suspenders, like a muffin baking over the sides of a pan.

"Hey, Rabbit, get me some jerky," he yelled through a bloody, flower curtain, the only thing dividing the shop and the butchering station.

Rabbit, who appeared to be more the butcher than Jack, brought him a piece of jerky. Scrap tried it. So did Randy. He nodded. Rabbit nodded. Randy nodded.

"Quarter pound," Scrap said as another truck pulled up and John Denver sang.

You fill up my senses/ like a night in a forest/ like the mountains in springtime/ like a walk in the rain . . .

Something in his voice made me feel both sad and hopeful, but hearing it in a butcher shop was like wearing a wedding dress to a funeral. It just wasn't fit for the occasion.

On our way out, a young kid dragged in a small stiff doe, looking like he'd searched the whole night through the woods for it. He looked tired and scared and almost sorry about what he did, but his daddy beamed.

Come let me love you/ let me give my life to you/ let me drown in your laughter/ let me die in your arms . . .

I wanted to tell the kid to enjoy his time with his daddy and not to scowl, but who was I to him to tell it? And I didn't know his daddy, but they were together and that mattered.

I fell asleep when we got back in the truck. I dreamed I was lost in a big city and every time I rounded another block, it was full of strangers too busy to help me. Animals were weaving through them making game trails. I tried to follow the trails because I knew they would lead me home, but they would always disappear, like down a pothole or into a bank. One led me to a prison that was surrounded by concrete and trenches and streetlights. A helicopter flew overhead blasting the theme music from Wheel of Fortune. I aimed a slingshot at it. I was wearing overalls and a dirty wedding veil.

I didn't wake up until Randy was gone and we were back at Scrap's. Someone had put a flannel blanket over me. It smelled like sawdust.

V

It took a minute before either one of us could speak. We just stared at the fuzzy little dog tied to the tree in Scrap's back yard. It stared back. There was a stale stillness to the air. The moon was gone, an owl moaned, a moth beat against the back porch light. Something was missing.

"What are you gonna do?" I asked.

He looked up at the sky as if it held the answer.

"Nothin'," he said and looked back down at the dog.

"But that's not Barry."

Scrap sighed.

"Nope, it's not."

The dog's eyes were half-crossed, it had an under bite like a backhoe, like it could dig out a trench. Its hair was matted with sticks and burrs and other indecipherable things. I felt sorry for her, not because she was ugly, but because she was so dedicated to it.

"You should call her Loretta," I said.

"Her?"

"I don't know. Looks like a girl to me."

"I've always wanted a Black Betty."

"She's got hardly any black on her."

"She's got some black."

I leaned in and she about took my nose off. There was a smidge of black on her, but I think it was a grease spot, or, from the smell of her, something worse.

"She's got more white," I said.

"Well, that's what you call irony."

Scrap opened a small metal garbage can, pulled out a bone and tossed it to her. She gnawed on it with a desperate hunger that the bone alone wasn't going to satisfy. He turned to go inside. That's when I realized what was missing.

"Scrap?"

"Mmmhmm?"

"The horse is gone."

He didn't even turn back around. He just slumped over and breathed real heavy like he knew what he had seen but didn't want to acknowledge it until someone else did.

"We come and we go. That's all there is to it. Horses, dogs, dads. They're no different."

I liked to think that a little more happened in between the coming and the going and that who came and went mattered. And I knew that one day I planned to go myself, leave this town and this road and this county, and I wouldn't be back except to maybe dig up some of Scrap's irises when they got too overgrown or to give Momma some money because she would need it. And I didn't like that anyone would just up and take what someone else worked for—horse or dog or whatnot or whatever Daddy was jailed for stealing. There's nothing that could change my position so easily that all I had to do was take in the night something that didn't belong to me to right it.

"That rich man took your horse, Scrap. I'm sure of it."

I said it like I was angry, but I wasn't angry. I was just tired, I think. Maybe I had just had enough for one day too.

If Scrap had heard me, he didn't let on. He went inside, closed the door and turned out the light. So I started the walk home as the sun rose up in a dirty haze over the bend in the road. Momma would be expecting breakfast soon and I had to get the water boiling.

Night Blooming Cereus

Milli had never felt settled. Instead, she felt plucked from some random time period and some random place that came either a century before or after her own. She didn't feel like a product of her time or of her place. It was a general uneasiness and unrest that woke her in the night like a stranger at the door wondering where she was and why she was and what she would become. It was like she was walking through the woods, following a trail that leads into a ditch, knowing she had walked through that ditch in that very same spot at that very same time of day and she could see the proof of it by the print of her boot from the day before, but couldn't remember when, exactly, she was there or what put her there in the first place. She had always felt foreign to herself and the world foreign to her, which is why, maybe, she was a waitress at Mojo's, but she couldn't even say that with any certainty. Maybe, after attending six years of college with nothing to show for it, she really just needed the job.

The locals considered the owner of Mojo's their first modern-day, foreign resident, despite that Milli had considered herself the first by way of her Polish ancestry and northern roots. Growing up in small town Newt,

Mississippi, with parents from upstate New York felt abnormal and outsiderish, so she surrounded herself with people and things that seemed more abnormal and outsiderish than she.

Most foreigners who came to Newt had simply meandered off the Natchez Trace to see what Newt, Mississippi, "Home of the Tank Fish," was all about, and they typically didn't dig much deeper than into the corner Amoco station where they would exit with a shot glass that read, "Newt, Home of the Tank Fish," with the image of a stuffed, shellacked salamander schlepping a hermit crab shell on its back. She supposed this was the hopeful outcome of a previous mayor's marketing scheme to get people off the Trace and into the Town because the Tank Fish was as bonafied as the jack-o-lope and not nearly as cuddly. But who was she to judge? She had the largest unicorn collection in three counties, from porcelain figurines she won at county fairs to mail order bronze sculptures with jeweled inlays. One was made out of rope. The word had spread about it, eventually earning her an invitation to display her collection at the Shiners' Annual Charity Show-and-Tell event. It took 13 refrigerator boxes to load them, 263 pieces in all to which she had since added 17.

"Do you believe in unicorns?" a lady with netted hair and painted brows had asked. She was showing a hairless dog, which she held under her arm like a wad of packed, gray lint.

Never being able to excuse or explain or even validate her habit, Milli answered, "I don't really believe in them, but I think it's ok to believe in the idea of them."

The woman puzzled on that for a moment, shifted her

lint from one arm to the other, and asked, "Why do you collect something you don't believe in?"

Milli shrugged, bit off a hangnail, and replied, "Hopeful, I guess."

And as she drove into the sky that evening on her way to work (because in the flats of Mississippi you always drove into or toward or through the sky as it intersected the horizon spiked with cotton and clay and neon signs), she was hopeful, as well, in her ability to make a decent tip, though she rarely succeeded. And the sky, itself, was in a strange mood, the color of eggplants and oranges with a solitary cloud hanging on like the last drunk at a party, when suddenly it rained—an unexpected and urgent *splattery blach!*—one big, confident cry immediately sopped up by the summer heat before Milli could turn on her wipers or curse the cloud.

She drove past Arlo's Brakes, his sign pulsating and buzzing like a cheap bug light. And she drove past Sid's Cheap Cigs and wondered if he was still giving away novelty lighters with the purchase of three packs of Luckys. She would check into that later, she told herself, while turning into the parking lot at Mojo's, her muffler blurting smoke, scaring off a group of lazy doves under the young magnolia out front. The building was once a Jack Pyrtle's Chicken, and it still had the wood-shingled roof, bright blue paint, and sticky bushes to show for it.

Mojo's offered a taste of authentic unfamiliarity in the piney, parking-lot outskirts of town, a quasi-exotic Mediterranean eatery that served falafel and gyros and taboule and other dishes that intimidated Milli to pronounce.

Mohammed (Mo) owned Mojo's. His partner, Joseph (Jo) ran off with a wad of cash from the till, along with the company wagon. And while secretly Milli admired him for that, Mo swore he'd kill him if he ever set foot back in town.

Milli parked next to Mo's truck and stepped out into the hot, Mississippi night. Hot meant heavy. It meant everything moved slower than usual, and when you walked outside, it was hard to find air to breathe that hadn't already been exhaled by someone else with catfish breath.

The parking lot had just been resurfaced, and it was still tacky and springy, like a hardened trampoline. The imprints of cat feet led up to the front door. She followed them inside and parted the coffee-colored beads, studded with tiny bells, which separated the empty entryway from the empty dining room. The walls were painted magenta, orange, red, and cornflower. The ceiling spun with black acrylic fans, reflecting like pinwheels in the dull shine of the linoleum floor. Dollar-store votives, plastic flowers, and mirrored elephants perched atop ledges and shelves with other cheap knick-knacks. The furniture was second-hand. The chairs looked as if they belonged in a moose lodge, and the white tablecloths were thin and lightly stained. Altogether, the mood achieved was one of forced sensuality, the kind you pay for through 1-800 numbers, but the smell (oh the smell!) was divine—fresh cucumbers and pickled cabbage and sugary baklava and all the spices Milli's mother had never used. The restaurant was thick with them—the only advantage to its poor ventilation.

Mo's own mother sat in the back of the kitchen, rolling grape leaves, a cigarette dangling from her mouth, the ashes hanging precariously over her homemade dolmada stuffing, her right eye squinting from the smoke, a red bandana tied on her head, covering the roots of her long silver hair. She wore a man's gold lion-head ring on her pointer finger and reminded Milli of a pirate. She spoke no English, just nodded and smiled, and Milli imagined she had secrets, old princess-pirate secrets about how she escaped a country cratered by war and lived off olives and tobacco and the desert and had prayed to a God from a book Milli had never read to protect her son on his journey to America.

If Mo had ever lived anywhere else, he was only betrayed by his accent and his white and brown wing-tipped shoes because he gravitated to all things American, playing, at all hours, the oldies station, which Milli had grown fond of, associating Little Anthony and the Imperials with curry and mint. On this evening, as she rounded the corner to the back kitchen, it was the Everly Brothers.

I need you so that I could die,
I love you so and that is why,
whenever I want you,
all I have to do is dream, dream dream dream . . .

Mo swayed and sung, peeling carrots over the sink. He smiled at her, his wide eyes the color of dried out moss, his hair black and thick. He looked at her in a way that made her feel like he was sizing up spoils, in a way that made her feel like he knew more than she would ever know, and that was ok. If he shared what he knew then she wouldn't have to work to learn it for herself, like the time she was tempted into the line of the prayer drive-thru at Christ Community

Church. She figured if she could get some quick Jesus like she could get her fast food, then she could save herself the trouble of faith and works.

When they asked her what she needed them to pray for, she said she didn't know, so then they asked what was troubling her in her life. What did she need help with? At the time all she could think of was the Latin test she was going to have to take the next day. So they prayed for intellect and wisdom and fervor to serve the Lord in her profession upon graduation, and they gave her a free tube of bubblegum chapstick with the Christ Community Church logo.

She took over for Mo, knowing that was what she needed to do, and stood over the sink, scraping carrots, uncomfortable in her shoes, which fashioned large, silver buckles that pressured her toes. She'd admit to taking too much pride in her appearance, pride in sacrifice of practicality and considered the bunioned feet of old women, mangled from years of heels and hose, a deliberate disfigurement, as if men would only love them by the arch of their toes or bulge of their heels or contour of their calves. And so she shamed herself for wearing the buckled shoes, until she felt a hand slip up the back of her shirt.

Mo's breath was warm and smelled of peppery cigarettes. He once said that love was easy, like a series of light and effortless breaths, so Milli took that as a hint to stay away from the hummus, figuring he might not fall in love with a girl with garlic breath. But whether or not she wanted Mo to fall in love with her, she didn't know. She probably just liked the idea of it.

When her first boyfriend told her she was too needy, she said, "Needy? I need you, like I need the sky, and I don't even need that but to dream to and water my begonias."

At least, that's what she wrote in her journal a few days later. She was never that well spoken or clear headed about what her needs were. At the time she knew he was right, but she didn't pretend to care, and she hadn't pretended to care much since, even when Mo slipped his foot forward next to hers and pulled himself closer. His mother in the corner continued to fold grape leaves like little burritos, never acknowledging them, as if her very existence on earth depended on the delicateness of her technique and preciseness of her folds, as if one more dolmada would pay the price of her son's freedom, so she would put every effort into making it count.

"Did you enjoy your time off?" Mo asked, his hands wandering wherever he wanted as Milli stared at her reflection in the stainless steel backsplash, like a lone stalk of corn hanging out in the back of a foggy field, one that the farmer missed and let stand there alone just to see how long it would take before it fell over.

"I wouldn't say I enjoyed it, not really, but I needed it, so thank you," she answered.

"Well, I told you I could've helped you move," he said.

"Yeah, but it was something I needed to do on my own," she lied. "You know that."

The truth was that she would've allowed any stranger off the street to help. Any person she didn't know would've sufficed. It was strangers she felt she could be the most intimate with because there was nothing between them, and when there's nothing between them, no history or understanding of who the other person is or what they care about or what they've done, then there are no expectations of how the other is supposed to be. Those are the people she would have allowed to pack her underwear and her memories because they wouldn't have the least bit of personal interest in or attachment to any of it. But strangers were hard to come by in Newt.

She had been living in her parent's house since they had divorced and moved, each, after 20 years, trying to get as far away from the other as possible. Now, the papers were finalized and the house was sold and Milli was temporarily displaced, the contents of her life stuffed into a 10 x 10 storage unit, #26, secured by a hot pink combination lock and a $35 deposit.

While packing, she found an old picture in the back of a drawer of herself at eight years old, beaming on the edge of a rocky lake in her green, turtle lifejacket holding a piece of soggy pizza in one hand and a fish basket in the other—a picture that her mother had taken at a moment of breathless excitement when Milli stood defiant and certain, an adult's yellow mask on her face, after having just set a goal for herself. She was going to catch a fish, and she was going to do it with pizza.

She was after a minnow that had escaped from its Baits Motel when she had opened the lid and dared the younger kids to reach inside, and then watched in fantastic terror as it flounced through small, clumsy fingers, slapped its belly on the water, and dove into obscurity. At that moment and at that time, she was simply going to get it back.

She couldn't imagine that the odds of catching it with pepperonis and olives were against her, but who was going to tell her? Who was going to tell her that the have-a-heart fish basket had holes that would harbor no fugitive minnow with any wits about it? Who was going to be the heartless buzz kill to question her unorthodox choice of bait? Not her mother, who had taken the picture with the whimsical amusement of an adult who indulged a child's unscrupulous heart. Not any of the other lake goers who were mending their hangovers as they swept Cheezits out of their boats and stocked their ice chests with bologna and juice boxes and beer. Not any of the five other children who had resumed splashing around, stirring up a blooming cloud of silt and mucking up the water.

Of course, she never caught the fish, and she felt she had been splashing around in mucked up water ever since. She blamed her mother for it. She blamed her for allowing her to harbor the belief in ridiculous things like unicorns and hand fishing and school and marriage. If she could just force herself to be more grounded, maybe she wouldn't be considering sleeping in her 10 x 10 storage locker tonight, or worse, at Mo's.

The coffee-colored beads chinkled and plinked. They had a customer.

They looked around the corner to the portly lady, thick with makeup and pretense, waving overzealously at Mo and ignoring Milli completely. It was Barbara Spatz, one of their few regulars. She owned Barbie's Shoes on the Square. The shoes she wore were always too small, and today hers were yellow. The heels were worn and her feet hung over the soles like cheese from an omelet. Clearly, she was trying to tempt a man.

"Hi, Mrs. Spatz," Milli said, tying on her apron.

"Now, dear, you know it's Mizzzzzz," she buzzed loudly enough for Mo to hear.

Her bust, neither round nor high, and outlined with a tight, turquoise, cotton button-down shook like gelatinous fruit when she walked. Surveying the room, she chose a table the same way she chose her entrée, by first scanning her options, which never changed, and asking for the recommendations, which she never took.

"Spanikopita is today's special," Milli said.

"Again?" she asked, taking her usual table.

"Again," she replied, standing there, shifting in her uncomfortable shoes while the woman perused the menu.

Ms. Spatz reminded Milli of her social studies teacher from high school, a self-appointed Mississippi Belle, despite that she was from Nevada. She would blot her lipstick on a used tissue that held other older imprints of different shades of her lips. And she would comment on the population boom in her small town and how someone from Jordan was living down the street and how she had never heard of such a thing, even though she was a social studies teacher.

But that was long ago, and Milli wished she didn't think about long ago. Thinking about it made her break out in hives.

"Dear, your neck!" Ms. Spatz exclaimed, for example.

"Would you like the spanikopita today?" she asked, her voice rising like the squeal of a steaming teapot.

Ms. Spatz bumped her glasses to the end of her nose and leaned in for a closer look.

"Perhaps you should put some cream to that," she recommended.

"They'll go away," Milli replied, the heat rising to her face.

But Ms. Spatz doubted her, looking as if her appetite had been spoiled.

Nevertheless, she sighed and answered, "I'll take the moussaka."

She always took the moussaka.

Milli hurried back to the kitchen.

"Moussaka," she shouted and grabbed a cold rag for her neck. "Why do you stay in this town, Mo?" she asked more angrily than she meant. "You could live anywhere. Why Mississippi? How does anyone end up in Mississippi? I mean, you could go back to Jordan."

"Are you kidding?" he laughed. "Have you seen the news lately?"

"Well, I almost went to Alaska after I graduated. I was going to work in a fish cannery and live in a cabin and write poetry and marry a fisherman."

She thought he would say something inspiring and deep about his selection of Mississippi, something she had heard others say about its gluttonous mud and satiated air and fishbowled delta and people so rooted to the earth that they seemed to be born of it like bolls of exploding cotton, something that that would justify her own purpose in the place.

But he just smiled while he prepped Ms. Spatz's plate and said, "You can't get WXKZ Oldies in Jordan."

Milli slumped. She didn't get it. Maybe, she thought, she wasn't worldly enough. Every day on her way to work, she would pass a highway sign that read, "Red Banks 62 miles", and she'd imagine the 62-mile stretch of highway between it and her. Loblolly pines. Pearly stars. Scavenging possums. It seemed remote and otherworldy, as if the banks themselves held secrets of the savage wars fought between conquistadors and natives who were slaughtered for the land that was now dyed red from the history of their blood and resurrected into pots and platters by contemporary connoisseurs of pottery, or as if two young lovers had dug their way out of punishing homes from under backyard basements and quarries to the refuge and relief of the highway where a friend in a car waited to drive them to Texas where they could find peace and anonymity. But then, one midnight, 62 miles away from home, Milli found that she had glamorized the pines, which were covered with kudzu, and the stars, which were blotched by the clouds, and the possums, which were rank, roadside carcasses. There was nothing in Red Banks, especially at midnight, not even red banks, which she figured would be piled up along the side of the highway like the scenes of red tide off Panama City Beach. It was like driving into a suburb called Oakland and finding all the oaks had been replaced by cheap Bradford Pears, or like hiking into the Chihuahuan desert of Arizona to camp out next to the prickly night blooming cereus to wait for the baring of a single, fragrant bloom but falling asleep too soon and missing the rapture as it opens and dies just before dawn. (She had learned about that event during her fifth semester of college when she had decided to be a botanist, which was after she had opted not to become a psychologist or a film editor.)

"I think you're just lacking direction," Mo told her once as she complained of her college tuition bill and despaired over what to do with the rest of her life. "I watched this show on National Geographic about dung beetles. They navigate by the light of the moon. Did you know that?"

"No, Mo, I didn't, and I would've really been ok with not ever knowing that."

He smiled. His teeth were large and white, in contrast to his rich, tan skin. She could hardly tell he was a smoker. His English was well pronounced. He didn't struggle with his words, but his r's and d's rolled heavily off the cusp of his tongue that often held her own.

"They travel by solar pulses. The Egyptians considered them sacred. My mom is Egyptian, you know."

"What's your point?"

"I don't know. I guess it's that if the dung beetle can do something so beautiful as to use the moon as its compass, somehow I think you'll find a compass of your own, something that will give you direction."

She imagined a giant compass in the middle of her chest, like a benevolent parasite, pointing her North to the narwhalian sea.

She delivered Ms. Spatz her dinner and stepped outside for a smoke. Mo had rinsed out a bucket of burnt lentils behind the shop, and a river of water ran through the parking lot and under her feet. Beetles tinged against the plastic parking lot light that reflected off the water and oil like a stand-in moon. A feral, orange cat squirmed under the dumpster for a snack or safety or both. Two owls echoed each other in the pines and reminded Milli of the night she drove home from work, the road calm and dark and deserted after a quick, hard rain that rose up as steam and created a foggy ecosystem of asphalt and clouds and moonlight. It wasn't until she had already driven over the owl that she realized what she had done and came to a dead stop in the middle of the street. Checking her rearview mirror she realized that she hadn't ruffled a single feather, as far as she could tell. It still stood upright, its feet firmly planted, as if waiting for the next challenger in a game of chicken. She felt her heart might either quit or explode for the beats it was giving her as she got out and crept slowly over to the bird, feeling like she was in a dream where she could do anything like swim the breaststroke through the treetops or fling her braided hair over a balcony or pick up small owls or talk to sheep, because she reached down and picked the bird up, both stunned by the event. The owl turned its head 180 degrees while in her clutch and stared at her blankly with yellow opalescent eyes, as if it too wondered if it were in a dream. Carefully, she placed it in the backseat of her car so she could take it home and nurse it back to health and set it free, but as soon as she began driving away, the bird came to, shocked out of its reverie, as Millie drove 45 down Mount Holly Road. Her quiet and stunned little owl metamorphosed into a something angry and wild, its three-foot wingspan flogging the windows in the back of her two-door Honda Civic, flailing frantically in an attempt to free itself. She stopped and opened the door, and it perched on her back seat as if to ask what took so long, and after a brief moment of disbelief and hesitation, it flew away.

Two days later, she found it dead in the road near the very same spot she had picked it up.

And as she sat there on the back steps of the restaurant, the fireflies glittering up the woods like fairies with Polaroids, she thought about that bird and her own patterns of self-defeat that she hadn't overcome, and if she didn't, her life would evolve into the pursuit of nothing worthwhile and she would end up sleeping in a 10 x 10 storage locker or at a guy named Mo's. So, Milli untied her apron, folded it, placed it on the steps, and looked back over her shoulder to the back door. She checked the knob and was grateful that it had locked behind her. She walked across the springy parking lot, traced a word in the dirt of Mo's truck window, and rode over to the cigarette shop for a tank of gas and some Luckys. She added to the mix her free novelty lighter. The wind blew it north like a compass, and she liked the idea of following it.

Mr. Nobody

They were all just waiting for him to die. In between slugs of coffee and sealed deals, cheap shots and upsells, like housewives watching cakes char in passive plots against cheating husbands, they waited for him to die.

Because there was no doubt, the man was dying, and not in the philosophical sense as in we are all slowly dying. No, he was 83 and surely dying, having spent sums of Medicare and his personal fortune on injections, lubrications, and radioactive pastes and pills for lymphoma and emphysema and dementia and who knows what else.

Yesterday, he lost his balance on the showroom floor and blamed it on the water cooler.

He was surely dying, but he was resolute in his defiance of it.

And everyone was just waiting.

Harlon was occupied often by the thought, his affect already like that of a funeral director's—soft-spoken and light-footed, his words consoling and deliberate. The son of a Southern Baptist preacher, he had absorbed many of his father's mannerisms as if, while he estimated the value of your trade-in, he also considered the potential of your heart and the condition of your soul.

He sold Cadillacs—Burt Orphington's Cadillacs—and it was Burt who was dying, and sales were slipping, and Harlon was out of hair paste.

It was 8:32, and he was two minutes late for leading the daily sales meeting—a basic responsibility as the general sales manager. But he had lost his way in an old hymn and a cream cheese bagel, and he despised the lunchroom where the meetings were held. It smelled of old bananas and burnt sausage and bleach, smells that leached into his suits, along with the perfumes of old women, and his cleaners had failed him again.

Harlon was always two or more minutes late for the sales meetings, and for Burt, this was a problem. Being late meant being unmotivated. Being unmotivated meant being an idler. Idlers were dead weight and pitched out, and Harlon had already been pitched once. So, Harlon set Burt's watch back over a year ago. According to Burt's watch, it was only 8:25, as two salesmen next to him at the table quietly discussed a goose.

"It just fell from the sky," Mark said. "I think it hit a cable or something."

"Where is it now?" Barney asked.

"Out front between the sewage grate and the crepe myrtle."

"Is it alive?"

"Barely."

"My wife loves goose."

"Well, you can't eat it. It's against the law."

"Who would know?"

"You can't eat the goose, Barney. Pearl's already called animal control."

"What a waste. I hit a turkey once in the Escalade and took it home. We ate on it for days."

"Turkeys aren't protected, geese are."

"But she's mad at me. If I brought a goose home, it'd sure make her happy."

"No one here has a happy wife, Barney, only happy ex-wives. "

Harlon picked a poppy seed out of his teeth, said a prayer, and walked in. There was a new smell in the lunchroom: urine.

He locked the door.

"Good morning, gentlemen," he greeted.

The men murmured. Burt checked his watch.

"I said good morning," he tried again, rising on his toes to meet his inflection. "Frank?"

"I said good morning, Harlon," Frank, the used car sales manager, grumbled.

"Yes, thank you. You're up for the positive thought of the day."

"Oh," he sighed, and stood, slump shouldered and grim. Digging into his pocket, he pulled out a scrap piece of paper that looked like it had been found at the bottom of a gas station trash can.

"One door closes, two open up," he read through his teeth. "Helen Keller."

"Thank you, Frank. I think you used that one last week, and it's just as inspiring today."

Harlon glanced around the room at the ties of his peers and felt reassured none were as classy as his with the yellow and blue diamonds. He bought if off a street vendor for five dollars.

There was a woman at the table. He glanced at her breasts.

"Now, the Burt Orphington Creed. Let's stand, altogether."

And they all stood, except for Burt, who was confined to a new wheelchair, which everyone knew not to acknowledge.

They recited: "One hundred percent floor activity control. One hundred percent meet and greet. One hundred percent demo. One hundred percent T.O. One hundred percent switch. Feed our minds daily with positive thoughts. All keys in keytrack. All trades to the back fence. Complete Autobase tool. Give perfect, gold-key presentation."

This creed was copyrighted.

If you had read Burt Orphington's self-published autobiography, which hit the floor last Christmas, you would've learned that he claimed to have invented the concept of the team meeting, inspired by a round of man-to-man with his twin brother, Butch, a basketball legend in Tishomingo County. To his dismay, a person of no relation, obviously simmering in the same pot as he, published the concept first, prompting Burt to copyright every original thought he had thereafter. It's rumored he has a large, expandable file of copyrighted thoughts in a safe deposit box at the First American.

"Mike, name the Five Tenets," Harlon continued.

"Self-control, abominable spirit—"

"Indomitable," Harlon corrected.

"Right, abominable spirit, perseverance, courtesy, and integrity."

This, too, was copyrighted.

"Thank you, take your seats."

He was grateful, himself, to sit, his feet always aching. Always tramping the lot. For twenty years, he had been tramping the lot. He needed Tina. He had gone too long between pedicures.

"Harlon!" Burt yelled, before he had reached his seat. "What do we got in new cars?"

"Our goal is 15 new and 7 ups, Mr. Orphington. We got ten new and three ups. We're behind."

"Goddamit! We're not going to be able to make it! We gotta sell more cars. My sinus infection is cleared up and I hit 90 golf balls. I can turn my shoulders all the way around now and when I do that you can see my belly button. I point my belly button right towards that ball and I haven't done that in years. I'm back! And we're gonna sell more cars, Goddamit! I'm gonna get some plastic containers to get all my different medicines in, you know the ones that Raymond and Rainbow get. Ain't that right, George?"

"I don't know what kind of medicines you get, Dad," George answered.

Harlon felt something brush the bottom of his pants leg under the table, and he thought for a moment that it was his dog sniffing scraps, but then he remembered that he wasn't home. He was here. He was never home. He was always here. And he wondered when he last fed that dog. He didn't even want it. He had just kept it out of spite.

"Well I'm tired of people thinking I'm an old man, 'cause I'm back! Now I'm gonna get with my comptroller and he's gonna figure out why our expenses are too high. If you make more gross, your commission should go down, right Kyle?"

One end of the table heaved up and from under it sprung Kyle, like a startled gopher—a shoe in one hand and a black eye. No one asked why he was under the table or why he had a black eye because people quit asking long ago why Kyle did anything. Working with Kyle was like staring at a roulette wheel, believing you knew exactly where the ball was going to land, until it jumped off the table and hit you in the forehead.

"Right, Granddaddy!" he yipped.

Harlon eyed Kyle's tie. It was a Joseph A. Banks, a classy tie.

"Kyle, what do you got to say?" Burt asked.

"Oh, I'm just glad to have you back, Granddaddy. That's all. Glad to have you back. I'm a handsome man. I haven't done shit this week. I'm just glad to be part owner of this place. Harlon said it all, Granddaddy. He's the man. I'm tellin' you, he's the man. Harlon, tell 'em what you got."

"15 new, 7 ups," he repeated.

"Service!" Burt blurted, the force of which threw his head back. "Brent, what do you got in service?"

Everyone looked around for Brent.

"Brent's not here, Mr. Orphington," Harlon answered. "He's out sick."

"Sick! I just got outta the ICU. I've been taking three or four Exlax a day and I've been shittin' all over myself. That's sick! I'm a survivor of lymphoma, and I'm a survivor of the worst sinus infection in the world. It was in my skull. My skull! I'm getting back up to 600 calories a day. I'm back! George, do I take one Annavert or four valiums or four Annaverts and one valium?"

"I don't know what medicines you take, Dad."

"Goddamit! I'm getting my keys back and I'm gonna drive my car. I just had a massage. They just bent me over a chair and I feel so much better. Kyle, what do you got for this group?"

"15 new, 7 ups?"

"We're not gonna make it with that! Goddamit, I'm back! You're all gonna be fired if you don't get off your asses and make some deals!"

Burt considered himself quite the motivational speaker. He said so on page 12 of his self-published autobiography.

"When this lawsuit's over –"

"Dad, we're not supposed to talk about that."

"And we don't have to pay 2.4 million dollars and –"

"Dad, positive thought, Dad. Positive thought!" a red-faced George, interceded.

Burt looked at his son like a stranger and his face would've contorted if his nerves functioned properly, but he was a proud man and frequenter of Cindy's Skin Clinic. So his body had to make up for the range of motion that his face lacked, and he shook in his wheelchair, cussing and carrying on in all kinds of unidentifiable ways. His voice, like that of a balloon losing air, blatted about the walls of the room until he collapsed into his chair, his eyes shut and mouth wide and fists gripping the armrests in a type of frozen cardiac arrest.

And the room went silent as everyone assumed the same

thing—Burt was dead. It finally happened. They had all witnessed it.

Kyle's mouth dropped and eyes welled. A string of spittle vibrated from his lips. Harlon bowed his head and thanked God. Frank texted his new wife.

George seemed to be the only one who could hear his father's chest rattle on like his own tenuous sense of self-worth. He knew his father wasn't dead, just an old fainting goat. Then, he twitched to prove it.

"Hallelujah, Amen!" the only woman in the room hollered.

"I got him! I got him!" Kyle heaved over the desk. "I'll wheel him to his office. Don't touch him. I got him. I always got him!"

Harlon put his hand on Kyle's shoulder.

"No disrespect, Kyle, but you need to take him out the back way," he said.

"Yeah, least time he woke up kickin' like a mule deer," Frank added.

"It's the medicine," Kyle huffed, his eyes bloodshot and darting.

"Well, it scares the customers," Harlon said.

"Agreed," Gary said. "Get Rainbow to help. If he wakes up kicking, he'll listen to Rainbow. Meeting's over."

The dealership resembled a futuristic antebellum home— Scarlett O'Hara meets George Jetson—with towering front porch columns reaching up to a white ceiling curved like the buttress of a UFO. The walls behind were glass and the floors were a reflective black granite with silver starbursts. Accommodations included the plush, leather seating of unlocked Cadillacs, roller chairs, and the used luxury of the service area. Two great oaks shaded the strip of lawn between the five-lane avenue and the crepe myrtles, under which now lay a dead goose.

Peach, the finance manager, followed Harlon through the showroom floor and back to his office. His real name was Dave, but everyone called him Peach on account of his orange hair and pink skin. Harlon thought he looked more like a nectarine. He had a concerning lack of facial hair.

"Did you hear that Burt called Rainbow from his cell phone in the bathroom stall the other day? Said he needed help wiping his ass."

"That's awful."

"I know. He called Maria first, but she refused to help him. Said she had done it once already and wasn't doing it again," he laughed.

"Well, she's the janitor, not the nurse."

"She cuts his toenails. It's not a leap to assume she'd help in the stall. I finally got it on my phone, her putting superglue in the cracks of his toes. Want to see?"

"No, Peach, I don't ever want to see that."

"And to think when Burt dies, George and Kyle get it all. Kyle's is gonna blow it, you know, the way he spends. What's he on anyway? He's on something."

"No idea."

"8.2 million, and that's just the life insurance policy. Damn, you know what I'd do for that?"

"Well, you know what they say—one door closes, two open up."

✳

"He won't die," Kyle complained, leaning back in his chair as he inspected his eye in a small, gold compact. "The old man just won't die."

"That's your granddad. You shouldn't talk about him like that," Harlon said, having been called to his office.

"Aw, he's mean. Everybody knows it. Everybody's just waiting for him to die. And now he's crazy, I mean, touched in the head crazy, valium crazy. He should be home, not on the floor everyday. Did you know that he came up here on Thanksgiving and just sat here? He sat in his office from eight until five and then had Rainbow drive him home. We invited him over, but he didn't come. Can you believe that? It's crazy. Sabine made cupcakes —Hello Kitty."

"I'll tell you what's crazy. He told me yesterday that if I don't sell 25 more cars, I'm fired."

"No, Harlon, that's the truth."

"I'm eighth in the nation!"

"No one ever won a race coming in eighth," he said, leaning across his desk, peering at Harlon without looking him directly in the eye, as if he were waiting humbly for praise for such a wise remark. His eye looked like the membranous innards of a plumcot.

He was a small man, the image of his granddaddy fifty years earlier, but with a twitchy nervousness about him, the kind that manifests only in boys handed great opportunities with no idea what to do with them.

"I'll tell you what. You come in first, and I'll have my daughter make you cupcakes."

"Tempting, Kyle, but I'm diabetic."

Harlon's daughter's were 13 and 16. They had never made him cupcakes. They lived in California with their mother who had aspirations, which included being another man's wife. He found the engagement ring in the trunk of her car.

"You left me alone," she said. That was her reason for the affair, as Harlan worked 70-hour weeks to provide for his family, so she could be a stay-at-home mom and teach music lessons on the baby-grand he bought for her, so she could have her Broyhill furniture and a house in the suburbs, so she could add to her teapot collection and buy a fuzzy, white, purebred dog. She complained, "You left me alone," and she took pictures of her cha-cha at 3 a.m. to send to the military man she met online.

She was Miss Arkansas runner up, 1992. He bought her a custom-made bra for that pageant. Saved his money as a bellhop so she could compete. She was Church of Christ and valedictorian. She had all the qualities of someone true, except that she wasn't true. Then, she got aspirations.

He looked at the picture of Kyle's wife on his desk in the sand dunes with their daughter. He couldn't remember his last vacation or why you take one or what they are worth.

"There's only seven days left in the month, Kyle. We're in a recession. I can't make the numbers."

"Can't never did. That's what Grandaddy always says, and look at him now. He's my role model. He wrote a book."

"You just said—"

"Everybody's talking about it. He was on Good Morning Jackson."

Kyle's mind was like a gnat, quick and random.

"Did I tell you I bought a cockapoo?" he asked.

"I thought you just bought one of those mini shepherds, the ones with the blue eyes."

"I did, I did, but my wife said he needed a friend, so I got him a friend. I got him a cockapoo."

"McQuinn told me once that he got a white German shepherd just so he could beat it everyday."

"That's racist. That's why he's at Mercedes now. Do you have any concealer?"

"Makeup?"

"Yeah, for my eye."

"No, Kyle."

"Really?"

"Really."

"Listen, I paid $1200 for this cockapoo. I'm picking it up tonight in my Rubicon."

Rubicon. Harlon had a Rubicon. It was in California.

"Do you know what Rubicon means?" Harlon asked.

"Sure, it's like a puzzle, like a Rubix Cube or like, uh, like Jenga."

He was continuously awed by Kyle's disproportionate lack of auto knowledge in relation to his paycheck.

"No. It's a point of no return, like a moment of truth."

"That's it! You're the man. How'd you know?"

"I used to sell Jeeps."

"Oh yeah, yeah, that's you."

"What do you mean?"

"You always know what to say. That's you. You're like the Lone Ranger, or like Mr. Nobody. Yeah, Mr. Nobody."

Harlon winced.

"That was a long time ago."

"People still remember those commercials. I was too young, but other people remember you. They come and they say, 'Hey,' that's Mr. Nobody.' And I say, 'Yes it is! He's Mr. Nobody.'"

He was general sales manager at Wynatt's Chrysler Dodge Jeep, and a different man then. Attractive and young and eager for celebrity to impress his wife, he agreed to a series of commercial in which he played Mr. Nobody. Mr. Nobody wore a black cowboy hat when he was on camera; otherwise, he was without it. He preferred not to mess his hair, which resembled black Christmas tinsel.

"When other dealers say, 'Nobody beats our prices,' I'm the Nobody they're talking about."

That was his catch phrase.

He knew he had a gift in sales when he was six and had conned a cashier out of an extra pack of Big Chew. By 19 he was selling wine coolers to high school kids out of the trunk of his Prelude behind the Big Star. He felt important having access to inaccessible things. He felt accomplished.

The phone rang. Kyle hit the speaker button.

"Kyle!" Burt yelled through the phone.

"Yes, Granddaddy. How you feeling?"

"I'm back, I told you! Where's Harlon?"

"He's here with me."

"Harlon!"

"Yes, Mr. Orphington."

"Get your ass in my office. Now!"

✳

Harlon's heart raced and skin flushed. He had been slipping gas in his car under dealership tickets while Burt was hospitalized. And he knew this was it. He was found out. Or it could've been an under-the-counter deal he gave to a wholesaler or the personal incentive he offered a widow if she agreed to figures, or it could've been the lunch he ate out of the refrigerator that wasn't his own. He'd been fired for less, once by Burt, himself.

He checked his reflection in the nameplate of Burt's door. He had been using the old tanning bed he had purchased for his ex-wife and appeared to have just returned from the Bahamas, a story he often used on customers, or guests, as they called them. He had told quite a few stories of lives he had never lived, of kids he had never adopted and land he had never purchased and places he had never traveled, the stories changing depending on cues from guests to breach any barriers in the way of making a deal happen.

He looked into the office next to Burt's. It was empty, except there was a new nameplate the door. Sabine Orphington. She was six.

He opened Burt's door and stepped halfway in. His feet ached, but he concealed it. The man could sniff out weakness like a new car smell. If he was fired again, as he was four years ago on New Years Eve, he'd just go to Little Rock, he thought. They liked him in Little Rock.

"Harlon!" Burt yelled.

"Yes, Mr. Orphington."

"What's that thing we get down the street?"

Here it comes, he thought. He's gong to play with me a little.

"Thing we get?"

"Yeah, down the street!" he banged his brittle, manicured hand on the desk.

"Uh, gas?"

"Gas? No, not gas, you idiot! I'm talking about that thing we eat! Down the street!"

Harlon stood there, blinking.

"The sandwich! What's the name of the Goddamn sandwich?"

"You mean the chicken wrap with ice cream shake you get every Saturday?"

"That's it! What's the name of it?"

"Chicken Caesar?"

"Chicken Caesar! That's it!"

He pulled the phone receiver off his lap, and yelled into it, "Get me the Chicken Caesar!"

He threw it off his ear like a pair of cold ear muffs and left it dangling by the cord. The office became quiet except for the rattling in his chest and squeaking in his chair. Burt rubbed a smudge off his desk with his elbow. Harlon wiped his brow.

"Well what are you standing around for?" Burt asked. "Go sell some cars!"

*

Harlon stood in the middle of the showroom watching a man in a red jumpsuit pick up the dead goose and put it in a trashbag. He assumed the man was from animal control but couldn't be certain.

He had read once that when a goose is injured, its mate flies down and stays with it. He scanned the parking lot, but this one was alone. Figured.

"Pete's back, Mr. Dickson," Pearl, the receptionist, said.

She was the only person in the dealership who called him by his last name. She was a classy lady, a childhood friend of Burt's with a natural, aged beauty under a cheap, blonde wig.

Pete was eating a donut in one hand and holding open his right eye with the other.

"Good morning, Pete."

"Morning, Mr. Harlon," he smiled through a powdered -sugar moustache.

"Cold out there today, isn't it?"

"Yes sir, it sure is. Don't mind if I have a donut, do you?"

"No, but I told you to ask me before you come in here and eat."

"Yes sir, but I couldn't find you. I ain't harming nobody."

"I know, Pete, but you got to go. You can get some coffee, but then you got to go. If Burt catches you, he'll call the police."

"He's dying, ain't he? I can smell death, and it's on him and he's doing it fast. He's competitive. He thinks he's better than us."

"Well, he bought that donut."

"And he'd take it away, a fifty-cent breakfast from a homeless man. Don't these folks know they can't store up no treasures here on earth?"

"No, Pete, I don't believe they do."

Out of the corner of his eye, Harlon could see Barney approaching fast, and he could tell he had a deal to work from the rhythm of his hop-step, which he called his success march. He was Harlon's least favorite salesman, a former "treeologist." And he had worked in the oil fields. And he had been a carpenter, a real hammer slinger, apparently, but now his neck didn't move, his vertebrae was fused, and he was a hydrocodone addict and compulsive liar.

He was the highest grossing earner they had.

"Hey, nice tie, Harlon," he said. "Hi, Pete."

"Hi, Mr. Barney."

"Say, Pete, you could get off the streets you know. You could work here. Just fix that eye. Droops when you let it go, doesn't it? You could shower up at Harlon's house. He's got no one there. Big house too. He makes a lot of money. Don't let him fool you. We had a one-fingered salesman once who broke records. Hell, I can't move my neck."

"I'm happy where I'm at, Mr. Barney."

"And where is that, exactly?" he asked.

"Exactly," he answered.

"You got a deal, Barney?" Harlon interrupted.

"Yeah, a good one. He's retired. Rich old man wants to buy his sister a CSV, gold ice, fully loaded. She lives in Florida. She doesn't want it, but he's gonna buy it. Hey, is that man taking the goose?"

He hopped off his toes like an old, rusty spring, tossed Harlon his sales folder, and scuttled outside, while his customer sat staring at the blank wall in his office, his foot taping to the Flock of Seagulls.

"Go on and get, now, Pete. I've got work to do," Harlan nudged.

Pete shrugged and got his cup of coffee and an extra donut. His right eyelid dropped shut.

"We're all dying, you know that, don't you Mr. Harlan?" he said.

"Yeah, I know."

"Some are just better at it that others."

The front doors slid open automatically for Pete as he took his leave. A blast of cold air swept the donut from his hand, but he picked it up, stuffed it in his mouth, and disappeared behind a car.

Harlon walked back to his office and sat down. His feet still ached. He slipped off his shoes, turned on the fan under his desk and opened the folder. No trade in. That was good. He didn't have to work with Frank. He looked at the numbers and ran the incentives through his head, noted competitor pricing. He grabbed his pen, thought fleetingly about Florida and about death, and got to work.

Nobody beats our prices, he said to himself, nobody.

The Sugar Pot

Momma says I have to go to Mrs. Verna's for sugar. She wants to make shortcakes for my brother and we're out. Mrs. Verna lives two houses down on the left side of Monk House Road, but our houses are far apart. A division of two houses on our road is like a well you can't see the bottom to. You can hear the water when you drop a rock into it, you know it's there because it always has been, but you can't see if for all the darkness.

Mrs. Lollie is one house down to the right on the other side of the road. You can see her house from our driveway, but Momma doesn't let me go there anymore. The houses on that side aren't spaced far apart. They've been there a long time. At least, they look like they've been.

Mrs. Verna is the only neighbor momma likes. Mrs. Glenda is snooty and Mrs. Georgia is a Baptist. The others she don't count.

"Verna knows you're coming," Momma says and hands me the sugar pot. "She'll give you two cups. Make sure it's two. That will give me a little extra just in case."

"Yes ma'm."

"Don't dally. I've got to get these done by this afternoon."

"Yes ma'm."

Momma can't drive. She's legally blind. She can see me and she can cook and she can see letters on papers with a magnifying glass, but she can't drive. That's why I'm going to get my hardship license. Daddy isn't excited at all about me getting it, but someone has to be able to get around when he's at work. Momma can't get us anywhere.

She used to say God forbid if something happened to us out here because there's only one ambulance in all of the county. She doesn't say that anymore because it already happened and nothing will change. That's the way it is because the commissioners want to keep the taxes low. They're all farmers and own lots of land, Momma says. In fact, one of them died last winter waiting on the ambulance. That still didn't make a difference. They just replaced him with another one like him.

Out here, people are solitary. Most don't ask for much but to be left alone, but it's the leaving alone that gets them sometimes.

Mrs. Verna's old. She's got three raised daughters all living in the city. Everyone around here is old. Not many young people move out this way. The schools are poor and the roads are rough and there's not much socializing, at least not the kind they're used to. They leave the city looking to start gardens and dig ponds and raise chickens. There's been a pioneer revival of sorts, Momma says, but people who have lived here the longest don't know what to make of it. City folk, whether they mean to or not, bring the city with them, in their materials and in their heads and in their cars and their expectations.

They bring McDonalds too. Momma says we've already got all the food stops we need—Sonic, Gurkins, Food Rite. Any more would just be clutter, but she bets her life they'll bring a McDonalds. She likes the small town ways, the clock at the top of the courthouse that chimes every hour at exactly the right time, the old, empty general store. She likes the emptiness, I think, but only a certain kind of emptiness.

*

The blue butterflies are out, stopping on every dead thing in the road. Loads of them crushed under cars because they can't seem to find their way to the ditches, although there are plenty of dead things in the ditches and beer cans and sugar water. I read once that our roads are butterfly roads too, that they'll fly the easiest way home, not through the woods or over bushes, not if they can help it. So, they get in trouble with the cars. Either they can't move fast enough or they're distracted by bright flowers and awful smells and orange basketballs.

There's a crack in the sugar pot the shape of a bobby pin like it's holding the pot together. I imagine it opening up like a sinkhole and me falling in it and no one finding me because no one would think to look in the sugar pot until it's empty and I'm dead.

I pass the white cross on the side of the road. People put out crosses where important events happen, important to them and hardly anyone else even though the world splits forever and time slows down. The white paint is peeling and the letters routed out aren't as clear as they used to be. The zinnias are falling over behind it—pink, crook-necked flowers stretching up to the sun one last time before the fall turns them brown. More butterflies.

They say I saw it happen. But all I saw were tires and birds and a cat running under a porch. That's all I saw. Sometimes the cat is orange, sometimes black; sometimes it's no color at all, just bones and teeth.

I look at roads differently now. I see the way they bend and who drives down them. I count the cars and memorize their colors. I know who waves and who doesn't. I know who throws their trash out the window and who puts their dogs in the front seat. I know how fast they drive and if they're on the phone. I know when the Wilson Well trucks run and what they carry on their backs. I memorize license plates.

The lid on this sugar pot rattles every time I take a step. I don't know why Momma didn't send me with plastic. I think she wants people to know we still have nice things, but Mrs. Verna already knows what we have.

Mrs. Verna's husband, Claude, always gives me junk he finds at garage sales and estate auctions—weird old things like Avon perfume in Irish Setter bottles and parts of bikes and wood shavers. He fills up his house with other people's histories and I wonder if he's ever seen the empty room in our house and I wonder what he'd make of it if he did. Would he want to hang all his bird pictures and boxed baseballs and mantels from old houses? He talks about the old days and how much better things were and why I should carry a gun. And I think the old days were yesterday but his are farther away when he was alive in some different, more imaginary way.

"I'm only twelve," I reminded him last time I saw him. "I can't carry a gun."

"I don't care if you're six. Every girl, woman, and child should be packing something. The world is changed and it ain't changing back. You can carry mace, I'm sure of that. Just ask your momma to get you some."

I nodded. I couldn't tell him that I'm not afraid of the world and I'm not afraid of dying. I'm afraid of other things, like tornados and I'm afraid of most dogs, but I'm not afraid of dying. Only people who are afraid carry their fears in their purses and pockets. Tomorrow is nothing yet.

*

Mrs. Verna has always reminded me of a catfish. Her lips are squished together and puckered as if they were caught in a meat press a long time ago. Her eyes are black and far apart and beady. Her hair is always pulled back tight in a bun, showing off her flat head. Her skin shines like she has some kind of oil on it that she puts on thick in the morning and by afternoon it's melted off.

"How's your momma?" she asks.

I wait for a water bug to slip out of her mouth.

"Fine," I answer.

"She making shortcakes today?"

"Yes, ma'm."

She swims from side to side in the kitchen like she's never been in it, like she can't find a single thing she's looking for.

"Did you know someone finally bought the Carlisle house?" she asks, glaring into a cabinet.

I lie and say I don't know, but I knew that the Carlisles had finally been run out of town. No one would have anything to do with them after their son was put away. Drinking and driving. They were bad from the very middle of them, like a rotten pit inside a peach making rings and rings of rot. I'm sure they never had any nice sugar pots. They probably kept their sugar in a paper sack in a shed.

"I hear the new owners are from the city," she keeps on. "Educated. I don't blame them for moving out here, if you ask me."

Mrs. Verna finds the sugar and takes the pot and put two cups in it.

"Want some tape for that lid?" she asks, trying to get it back on solid.

"No, ma'm. It's fine. I've got to get back."

"Ok, I'll see you next Saturday at the pancake breakfast at the firehouse, right? Your momma said y'all were coming."

I shrug and walk out. I don't want to see them again. For three years I've had to go to that breakfast. I don't like anything about it. The sirens and the speeches and the hung looks and the sorries. It makes me angry, nothing more, just angry. Making a production about saving lives and risking lives over a plate of pancakes. Not everyone can be saved.

I don't think there's a single straight road in this whole town. I used to get sick in the backseat of the car on the way to school. Daddy would have to drive real slow or let me sit in the front seat and Mathew would roll his eyes like I was making it all up. These roads. You think you're getting somewhere and then you hit another curve or dip or hill you can't see over and you're still nowhere at all.

I walk by a pasture with a smokestack and no house. It's been burned down for as long as I can remember. I wonder where the people went. Did they die? Did they move? Did they go to pancake breakfasts? Did they have kids?

A horse chestnut tree grows from the concrete slab where the house once was. Its ugly, green fruit has dropped. Life continues in the strangest ways.

A squirrel darts across the road and Mrs. George's rat terrier barks at me with all his body from his front porch. I think that one day that dog will burst inside itself.

I walk faster, the lid clanking, my hands sweating and before I even know it, I slip on some loose gravel and drop the sugar pot into the ditch. It breaks so easily, like an egg in the sink and my eyes quit working and my breath leaves me. I can't see the pot or the sugar or the weeds or the trash in the ditches anymore.

I see the gulf. I see Mathew at the beach, his hair curly and brown catching the wind and spinning and whirling like colored oil in water. He smiles at me and holds up a shell, but I can't see it in the shadow of his hand. I can never see it, but I can hear the gull wings on the wind and someone's muffled radio and each bead of sugar spill out, like sand through a steel funnel, like the sand we played in and the shells that jangled in the waves. There were so many after the hurricane and the red tide that summer—conchs and tiger claws and scallops and the popping of air bubbles from thousands of tiny clams burying their bodies after each wave dragged them out of the water.

I sit in the ditch and cry so that no one hears me and so that everyone can, but I can't let momma know. I won't let her see me cry. She'll see me be the one who comes home. I can't go back to Mrs. Verna's, though, I just can't. So I scrape up the broken pieces, wipe my face with my shirt, and head for some place more familiar.

Mrs. Lollie's house is beige, just beige with a thin, gray roof and pots with half-dead plants. She's got a metal glider rocker in her yard, a card table set up for Sunday dominoes and a propane tank. Her driveway is close to the road and gravel and there are tokens of people in it—cigarette butts and beer tops and plastic bits. I knock on her screen door. It's been scratched up by the cats. She always has a yard full of cats. The basketball goal has lost its net. Weeds are growing up around it. Momma never would get Mathew one.

I hear her coming before she gets to the door. She isn't a small woman. She fills her whole house with her own body and on Sundays with all sorts of family.

"Well, Miss Sophie Rose, my Lord, come on in girl, come in," she smiles.

Her smile never changes. It always surprises you with its size and its goodness and its ability to put a lightness in your heart that you sometimes forget exists because you've felt heavy for so long. There are some places that just feel like that, like home, no matter if good or bad things happen inside of them, like how the smell of cigarettes and beer remind me of my daddy. I know they're not good. I know they're vices, like Momma says, but they're him and they're home. With Mrs. Lollie, it's her smile and her bigness and her always having food made and her apple cinnamon candles.

She looks down at the pieces of my sugar pot and I suddenly wish I had pockets.

"What you doing with that broken thing, child? You ok? You cut anywhere?"

Her eyes dart up at me. They are kind and brown and worried. She's always ready to put a band-aid on something. She's never gentle about it, but she goes about it as if her sole purpose in life had been leading up to that most important moment where she had no other mission but to dress your wounds.

"No, I'm fine. Do you have any sugar?"

She looks at the pot like I think she wants to look at me, with some sort of sorry. She is a tall woman with skin the color of soft, wrapped caramel. She wears a gold turban and red scarf and a shirt with sleeves that billow out like chefs' hats.

"Of course I have sugar, child. You sit."

She puts me at her table and sets a water to me. She moves through her cabinets with a slow purpose and draws out what she needs one by one. I look around her kitchen for anything new because that means time has passed, and I wish time was a lie, but the second hand that ticks like a freight truck on her wall clock puts me in my place.

"You're growing up, Miss Sophie Rose, turning into a fine young woman. Would you'a guessed I'm 72?"

"No, ma'm, not at all," I answer.

"How much sugar you need again?"

"Two cups."

She pulls out a large aluminum container and puts three scoops into a plastic bag and hands it to me.

"A little extra for you," she winks, and hands me another plastic bag. "Here put your broken pieces in this bag, unless you want that I help you fix that pot. It don't look too broken."

"That's ok. Momma will know I broke it anyway, so it won't make a difference."

"Well, looks like it was a mighty nice pot, but I don't think she'll be too sore, considering." She pauses and looks at me like a puzzle she has lost a piece to. "How is your Momma?"

"Ok, I guess."

Then she looks at me like to ask me the same but knowing I'll lie, so she doesn't ask and I don't say. She takes me to her and puts her arms around me and it feels like being wrapped up in blankets, just piled on and on so I don't have to get out from under them again if I don't want to.

"I still can't believe it happened here," she says.

And she smells like grass and grease and apple cinnamon and I want to stay there and kill the clock and eat the cake sitting in the corner of her counter. But I have to go.

*

I used to think that when Mathew died that his body was covered with all those blue butterflies on the side of the road, that they were there to carry him to heaven, that they must have a secret purpose like that. But those cars. They just keep coming and running them over. Over and over and over. And I wonder why they don't learn, why they don't get out of the way because the people in the cars don't stop or look or turn around. I see the Carlisles in every one of them.

I step on a butterfly to see what will happen. Nothing does. Another one just comes and sits on top of it, like they do all dead things, for no other reason than to be a little higher up off the ground, I suppose.

Sometimes I feel like I've been born with an open wound. It scabs over and the butterflies land on them, but then people pick and pick at it and it bleeds. It seems like it will never seal back up. It just bleeds. And it's somewhere real prominent, like on my face, so I can see it every time I look in the mirror and so can everyone else. They never see me.

Walking back down my driveway, I wonder what the time is. I only know it's not past one o'clock yet. I know that from the route of the sun and the shadow of the tulip poplar and the path of the buzzards in the sky and Mrs. Lollie's clock. Each second, for the rest of this day, will become a lifetime lived and died, over and over, and Momma and I will make shortcakes for Mathew because they were his favorite. We won't eat them, but we still have time to make them, and the dough will rise in the oven like new breaths.

The Free Bird

The sign read Free Bird. It didn't specify the species. It was free and Eula rarely passed on a bargain. The sign was painted on a cardboard box and fastened to the grass with a spear of rebar. She wondered why someone would give away a bird and why this person was so vague about the offer.

She had, what she considered, a good sense of fair transactions, having learned such from her dad, who had secured a stockpile of weapons, musical paraphernalia and collectibles. It was better to put money into tangible things than give it to the government or lose it in a 401K, those were his beliefs, things that would supplement his income in a pinch. The pinches always came, like when he went bankrupt stockpiling for the pinches.

But he was a stupid man and none of that mattered now.

Eula was the only accountant in three counties who made house calls. Homebound clients tended to stay homebound and she liked that security. She charged a travel fee of $25. When gas prices were high, she added an Overabundant Fuel Exhaustion or OFE surcharge of up to twenty percent. Because most of her clients were rural and the distance between one and the other protracted, she felt justified in this.

It was on her way to an appointment with Mrs. Ida Ruth that she passed the sign for the free bird. Mrs. Ida Ruth was 92. She kept her business receipts in a denim bag stitched with the words Random Crap. Her business was resale. When her knees quit working, she fronted the lower great-great generation of her family the money to make purchases at trailer auctions, garage sales, and junk stores to then resell on EBay or in her storefront Mrs. Ida's You Name It Store. She subsisted through their hard work and, to her vehement attestation, the Grace of God.

"You know who woke me up this morning?" she asked after Eula settled into her aluminum kitchen chair.

"Yes, Mrs. Ida Ruth, I know who woke you up."

"You do? Who then? Who woke me up?"

"I know."

"I want to hear you say it."

"God."

"Yes, Gawd! Gawd woke me up this morning. He woke me up again! It's a blessed day!"

She took a pile of papers from the plastic card table and she shook it. It was a bible, the cover gone and spine loose and pages bent and warped like it had been dropped in the tub. It was the most used bible Eula had ever seen, only having reference from the one stored with the cookbooks at her parent's house.

She wondered if her dad had ever read the thing. If he had, would he have changed his mind?

Mrs. Ida began with that bible every time Eula came over.

"Everything you ever need to know about the world is in here. It's all here. B-I-B-L-E. That's the book for me! You don't need no education. People go and get degrees and don't know that it's all right here. Every answer to every question. There's even airplanes in here. Did you know that? Just look. They're in here."

Eula nodded. She always nodded.

"You get down on your knees every morning and thank Gawd he woke you up. If your knees hurt you sit on your bucketocks. You know where your bucketocks is?"

Eula nodded again.

"If your bucketocks hurt, you lay on your back. If your back hurts, it don't matter. You can thank Gawd anywhere, even driving down the road. And love your enemies, Miss Eula. I had a woman once tell me she wanted to cut off my head and she also said something about my bucketocks but she didn't use that word, you know. I had to love her. He said I had to."

Eula couldn't think of any enemies of her own. She thought back to the bird. The last time she got something free it cost her ten dollars.

"Can you do six?" she had asked the man at the junk store.

He paused, thought about it, and took a bite of a cheese sandwich.

"Naw, ten dollars, that's what I paid. That's the best I can do."

She looked down at the old mailbag. It was big enough to fit a small child, but the leather handles were eaten away.

"Well, how much for the Texadillo?"

"I'll throw that in."

So she walked away that day with a mailbag, a Texadillo penny bank from the Texas sesquicentennial, and a sledgehammer for her dad that she gave another ten dollars for. The man said he could get that selling it for scrap.

She wondered about that sledgehammer. She didn't see it when she cleaned out the garage.

Mrs. Ida Ruth was always quick to deal in the parable of the rich fool with Eula but she figured that was just because she wanted her to cut out her travel surcharge, as she did on this day.

"I'm a business woman just like you, Mrs. Ida, and I'm offering a service few others will. For that, there is a slight fee to cover my personal time and expenses."

"How 'bout you just take this here magic picture lantern Sissy got at the Miller auction?"

"You know I don't barter. I might need your help selling some things, some of my father's things, though."

"Oh, bless your heart, child."

She looked at Eula like at a wounded dog.

"Well, we can discuss it later. I'm going to take your receipts here and I'll be back next quarter."

"Only if Gawd wakes you up you will!"

"Yes, Mrs. Ida, only if God wakes me up."

She took her bag of Random Crap and left.

*

She worried she might be too late. The number of cars that passed the sign was considerable, but the driveway itself was a treacherous strip of gravel and dirt and weeds with a steep incline.

They had few hard winters but she still wondered at the practicality of such a driveway and the wits of the person who lived at the top of it. The ascent was dented with craggy potholes and washed-out sloughs her Camry wasn't designed to handle, so she dredged the outskirts of the weeds.

At the summit was a small, white house, one that might slide down and settle into a better place, like the middle of the road, if not for a wisteria bush in full bloom that tangled into its eaves and propped it upright. Next to the house a green metal structure kept the rain off an old truck and next to that a brown metal storage shed.

This is why she preferred the suburbs. Paved driveways, tidy bushes, leveled roads. She knew what time her neighbors went to work, the mailman's route, the temperaments and names of all surrounding pets, the acceptable height of the grasses per the HOA, where to look out for children. Suburbs were safe, well lit, accessible.

She parked her car next to a pile of rotting railroad ties.

A thin man with a gray beard and ponytail met her outside. He wore jeans and rubber slides and a Bozo's BBQ t -shirt.

She informed him she was there for the bird.

"Alright, I'll go get it."

He disappeared around back and returned with a cardboard box punched with air holes.

Her dad would have been proud of her getting something for nothing, but why did she care? He was a hard man, and in the end, a selfish one too.

"Took me a minute to get her out from under the house. She likes her freedom."

He opened the box to a wad of feathers and defeat.

"It's a chicken," Eula said.

"A silkie hen."

It was missing a couple of toes and one eye had a film over it.

"A birth defect," he said.

It was also molting and a coon had gotten at it a month ago, but he considered her a loyal companion and good layer.

"Lays the most perfectly shaped eggs you've ever seen," he said, "and you can hold her like a baby."

"And she's free?"

"Yes ma'm."

"What do you feed her?"

"You can buy layer pellets at the co-op or you can let her loose to eat off the yard. You can give her nearly all kinds of scraps too. She's a natural composter. You into organics?"

"No," she answered.

He shrugged and placed the box in her front seat. Before she left, she gave him her card and then drove to the city pet store for supplies, careful not to take the corners too sharp.

The clerk at the pet store said they didn't have anything for chickens, that they only dealt with domestics. She pointed out the lizard behind him, basking under a heat lamp.

"You mean that thing is a domestic?" she asked.

"Well, you know what I mean."

"I would think that chickens would be the most domestic of all. We grow a billion of them a year."

"We don't eat our domestics."

"I'm not eating my chicken."

He shrugged.

She noticed two twitching antennae beetling from behind the lizard's rock.

"What about crickets?" she asked.

"We don't eat those either," he grinned.

Eula, who wasn't gifted with a sense of humor, grew impatient.

"Really, this shouldn't be that hard," she huffed.

"Ok, aisle eight. You'll find the crickets on aisle eight."

She found them on aisle seven, and on her way back to the counter, grabbed a pink puppy harness and leash. Careful not to instigate further conversation, she placed her business card in the jar on the counter for a free door prize, purchased her items, and left. After tussling with the bird in the parking lot, she secured the pink harness and leash and placed it back in the box.

$*$

Her plan had been to drive back to her office, a small two-room space she leased next to the Hair Gallery, and put the chicken in the bathroom. Instead, she drove north, away from the town and out to a yellow house on Quail Hollow Road. She idled in front of it.

Her dad's truck was still in the carport, the lawn mower beside it. Stupid man, she thought. Bet the sledgehammer's there.

There was corn everywhere. She was confounded by the amount of corn farmers grew. Wild dirt manna, there it was, always growing, every summer, more and more packed tighter and tighter. She didn't even like corn.

This living out here, she thought. It didn't make sense. It was so far from things.

"He'll be back," her mother said. "He always comes back."

But he died in the dirt in front of that yellow house. He had died and they didn't even know it.

The sun dipped two degrees. The clouds were pink and orange and yellow. The sky was purple.

A woman looked through the curtains.

The chicken scratched in the box and cooed.

Eula looked up and down the road. Nothing but corn and martins and sky and this yellow house. She placed the car in park, leaned over and opened the passenger-side door. Gently, she turned the chicken box over and watched as the bird fell out and ran into the cornfield, the pink leash trailing behind her.

She looked at the bag of Random Crap she had tossed on the floor, turned around in the driveway, and headed back to her office, crickets chirping in the backseat.

Cinderblock Houses

My grandma, my mother, and I live together in a cinderblock house at 57 Bethel Road. Grandpa used to live here but he died a year ago. Influenza.

"I opened up the window and in flew Enza."

The house still smells of him—the ground chew he used to suck like licorice. I would sit on his lap and he would bounce me on his bony, crooked knee, or nibble my ear with wet lips just before spitting phlegm and tobacco into the Foldgers can. On the floor. Next to us. We sat together in his worn, green rocker, a rocker as bony and crooked as his knee, and we cautioned the wind and the weeds not to blow so hard or grow so high.

*

I wish I were a crow

watching golden corn grow all day

but I am

*

Mom sits, now, in Grandpa's worn, green rocker, and rocks and scratches and shifts. She's always shifting, crossing her legs. Dangling shaky feet. Making noises with her slippers as they slap at her heels and scrape the floor.

Her birthday is coming up. July 4th. She gets lights on her birthday. Grandpa and Grandma always told her that on July 4th everyone from all over celebrated her birthday, and she believed them. But it's a hard thing to prove otherwise, especially when she only ever asks for the lights or salt and pepper shakers. And she usually gets one or both. But I think she would like some new slippers this year, although I'm not sure. She likes the way these feel against her cheeks.

*

I brush her hair in the mornings when she is up and I'm not late for school. Since it's summer now, I brush her hair almost every morning. Sometimes, she grins at me when I do, but most of the time she doesn't.

She sings.

Don't sit under the apple tree with anyone else but me, anyone else but me, anyone else but me.

Her hair is longer than mine, to her shoulders, but it's dull. Brown and odorless. Strings break off in the brush and I wish I had known her when her hair was young and her face was full.

I'm sure it wasn't my fault being born. If I could have I would have gone back into (in two) my mother's womb. I would have kicked harder and harder until her belly, bruised and busted, and her brain, sore and sorry, would have turned on me. She would have turned on me and knifed herself just to get rid of me. But I was too quiet in there, too still. She says I was "like a little pink owl. You were turning 'round in there so softly, rubbin' my belly to sleep, and I would wonder who, who you were in there, Little Owl, who."

And now, we have cable for her. She likes the home shopping network. Grandpa didn't want cable, so we didn't get it until after he died. He said that it would give us too many excuses to be discontent. I think he may have been right. Mom rocks faster than she used to.

✳

So it's morning, and Grandma's frying sausage again. Mom loves sausage, but I think it stings going down. Grits are better. The oven vent is rumbling, sucking up the steam and grease since the cinderblocks don't. Often I've wondered where it all goes, like bathtub water and garbage. It just goes.

I used to be afraid of the bathtub drain, that it would suck me down there, that it would strain my body like spaghetti and instead of just one of me slipping through the drain there would be twelve. But I've never been afraid of the trashman. He has a nice smile.

✳

Caroline's come over. I can tell its her because she has a special knock.

1 ~ 2 ~ 1 ~ 2 ~ 3

"Wash your plate and you can go out and play," Grandma tells me.

Caroline knows to stay outside and wait for me.

"And wipe off the table. It's all sticky now."

I slop the aluminum table with a dishrag and throw it across the kitchen into the sink, fluffing Grandma's hair a bit. She squints her eyes—filmy eyes—at me, but looks to the back of my mom's head in the rocker, and softens—gazing eyes. So I run.

∗

Down the cinderblock steps, Caroline's putting the pieces of her clarinet together, leaning against the birch tree. She flips the clarinet reed sideways with her tongue. She accidentally swallowed the reed once, but it came back eventually. That happened to a cat I had too, only with a bell.

"You wanna walk over to the pond," Caroline asks, the reed hanging from her bottom lip.

"Ok."

There's a breeze I don't feel tangling Caroline's orange hair, twisting it into all sorts of curls and directions. But she tosses it back, puts the reed into the mouthpiece, and begins to beat a series of hard notes.

The notes are gone almost as soon as they've come. Noise is hard to follow outside of the house, back in the pastures. In some places the grass is as tall as me and grabs at my clothes or pokes my knees (kind of like the kids at school). But I poke back or rip them out of the way or mash them down, because I can do that . . . to the grass.

There used to be a fox that lived back here. He made trails in the grass that Caroline and I could follow. That fox took us all sorts of places, good places, and I wondered if he knew us, if he brought us on purpose. Last summer the pond dried up, and the flattened trails the fox had made began to stick back up and grow into the tall pasture grass, becoming harder and harder to follow. We thought the fox was trying to lose us, that he wanted to be left alone. But one day Caroline's brother heard noises coming from the old well behind their house, and he looked down there and there was the fox. He was *all bent and crying*, her brother said. So he picked up some big rocks and threw them down there.

Stupid fox. He didn't know what else to do. Neither did Caroline's brother. When Caroline found out what her brother had done, she screamed and shook and threw her clarinet at him. But later she went back to the well and threw some flowers over the stones . . . over the fox.

And she named him Perdy.

"If there had been any water in that old well, that fox sure got it," Caroline told me.

When I get back to the house, my t-shirts are hanging from a wire in the backyard, and a red-breasted bird is wailing from the top of the shed. The roof is made of green plastic that looks like it's see-through but it only lets the sun and clouds in. It looks like a frozen green sea with frozen green waves, and it's patched together with wood and shingles and rusted nails. The sides are thick, black, and sandpapery, but the roof isn't. Grandpa's doing. He was a sucker for cheap materials, Grandma said.

On my way around to the front door, I pluck a couple

of honeysuckle growing on a bush under the living room window, and I bring the flowers in for my mom.

*

Grandma invented this grand story about my dad. She begins the story the same way every time I ask her to repeat it, and I ask her a lot. She takes my head between her hands and buries it in her plump breasts. I have never seen her eyes during these storytellings. I have only felt the shortness of her breath, and vibrations of her wheezing. The more she tells it, the more difficult it becomes for me to hear it, as though each time she buries me deeper and deeper into her, and my face creases in her cleavage. It is as if she wants to put me back in a belly, her belly, so that I would never have to hear the lies (I know they're lies.)

> Her many short breathings ~
> awkward, rhythmical
> are like rusted hinges
> slamming shutters.
> I shudder.

"Your father was a fireman" (criminal) "handsome" (oafish) "chivalrous" (perverted), a man who was killed" (jailed) "saving" (hurting) "the life of a child just about your age."

*

This house is always cold, even in the Mississippi summers.

And so I sit. On the floor. In the sun. Where it's warmer. Beside my mom. And I watch things flash across the television screen.

I never sit in front of my mom. I can't tell where she is.

The sun moves across her slippers, across the floor, growing long, narrow, sharp. A fly spits in and out of the light, mixing up the dust and the dreariness. Sometimes it hits the window, and that throws it back a ways.

There are hot spots in certain places in the hall—in the hollow hall of the house. I wish I could pocket one and take it out when I get into the living room. Or the kitchen. Or the bathroom. Take the hot spot out and wrap myself up in it. But instead, when I find one I have to stand. In the hall. By myself. And stand, crumpled up, with my shoulders and my neck drawn in. Crumpled. And crouch against the rough plastered wall.

*

Grandma says that if I stick my lip out much farther someone is liable to trip over it. I ask her WHO. She just smiles as if she knows who but won't tell.

*

And this house keeps in odors.

If it were round and if there were a hole in the middle of the roof, maybe it wouldn't be able to hold onto these odors so tight.

But I live in a rectangle.

And there's a door and there are three windows. One is nailed shut. So this house keeps in odors. The bread basket smells like sausage and the kitchen sink like mildew and milk.

*

At the pond, sitting on a brittle stump, Caroline had asked me if my mom ever yells at me.

"No."

"Does she ever say that she'll send you away?"

"No, not really." I hadn't been asked to go anywhere away from the house, but since Grandpa died I haven't felt like hanging around much, at least not with Mom, which isn't the way it always was. It's just that Grandpa was always there to make up the difference.

"That's good," Caroline said, polishing her clarinet with her shirt. "Sometimes my mom says she'll put me away."

"Where do you think she'll put you?"

"Sometimes she puts me in the closet, but I don't think that's where she means."

*

Caroline lives about a half-mile to the left down Bethel Road. She has a brick house. Brown. And a porch. She has a dad that I have never met. But I know he's there because I've seen his boots.

Caroline rides her bike over to my house most of the time, rides it despite the worn, crumbling road connecting us.

The pastures end behind my house. End before her house. When we don't walk, and when she doesn't have her clarinet or sometimes even when she does, we ride our bikes through the pastures, dodging rabbit holes and rocks. Up and down, down and up over the hills, over the hill, over the . . .

And sometimes we go to the pond; sometimes we don't.

✳

Caroline's thoughts are so good. It's as if they're packed in boxes and padded with clouds and kittens, and on the boxes are the labels FRAGILE, THIS END UP.

And when a boy at school once said that my mom was crazy and my dad was dead, she blew her clarinet in his ear so loud that he ran away. Caroline doesn't seem to be afraid of much.

The day school let out for the summer my teacher told the class to write down all the things we loved about summer vacation. I thought of many things, like Caroline and sprinklers and fireflies. But I only wrote down the one thing that I loved most about summer vacation—no school.

I could do without most of it, except for Caroline. She stays by my side at school and we go places together—lunch, recess, the bathroom.

✳

I don't like going places with Mom. I won't go places with her anymore.

"Wipe it!"

She yelled at me at the last open house. In the bathroom. The bathroom smelled like lemons and vanilla musk, and she looked in at me. There were no locks. There never have been. Her cracked hand gripped the cracked door and held it open.

"Wipe it!"

Grandma knew not to let her out like this. Mom didn't take her medication right that day and there were people around. But I wasn't thinking about the stares, the upturned upper lips showing teeth like irritated dogs. It was her hand, her fingernails, split and rigid, landscaped with cacti, barren. Gray grit showed through. Her cracked hand gripped the door so steadily. Still. Tight. Her knuckles turning from red to white to yellow as she dug into the door.

"Get your pants up girl! Come on!"

She was slurring her words when finally Grandma came in.

"Hattie, shhh, not so loud," Grandma said. She was nervous and smiling at the stares, but Grandma was used to it.

Mom grunted from some place deep.

"Hattie, dear, close that door, now. It's time for us to go."

Grandma didn't have to ask Mom again. She held her arm and then her hand, leading her away from my door. Mom's eyes were clouded and lost to me, and even to herself, and I was out of the bathroom before I had to look at them. She used to have Grandpa's eyes. Light green eyes outlined in black, eyes that could keep you looking back because they seemed hollow and endless. I used to look in them and try to find things she knew or things I had lost. When I lost a doll, I thought I could find it somehow in there if I kept looking deep, deeper, but her eyes worked like a vacuum, always absorbing, extracting, inhaling, anything you didn't want.

But now, they don't even do that. They just sit in sockets and rock back and forth with her in the chair.

*

It takes a bit of effort to get to Grandpa's grave. He was cremated so he could be scattered places in death he could never have been in life. We still have most of his ashes on account of we haven't been able to make it to a few of those places yet. I wouldn't know how to begin to get to Saskatchewan or The Canyon.

Grandpa only took two vacations in his life; one to Atlantic City for his and Grandma's tenth wedding anniversary; and the other to see Uncle Larry, Mom's brother, in Spur, Louisiana. But he never considered that one a vacation. They say I went, but I don't remember.

And I remember a lot about when I was four, mostly about my Grandpa or my accidents, like when I scarred my knee on the wooden wheel at the end of our driveway. But I don't remember going to Uncle Larry's.

I remember when Uncle Larry came here. To Grandpa's funeral. And I remember wondering if his shirt was going to hold in his belly. Between his coughing and chewing, he had stretched the shirt and its buttons past their limits. He had rings, pools, under his arms and always a handkerchief in his hand to smear his chest and forehead. He had pride, only it took on forms other than hygiene.

*

"Yeah, and he was just a staring at me the dumb shit, oh, sorry Mama, and I was thinking just stay where you are pretty boy. Oooh, he looked so good, I could just taste the stew and steak I was gonna get off that boy. And we looked eye to eye, and he knew his time was up cause I had that barrel aimed right at his chest, and BABOOM! He was mine. He laid flat out on the ground with his neck flopping and his tongue hanging out, and I'll be damned, excuse me, Mama, if his heart wasn't still beatin' when I started gutting him."

He rocked hard and panted hard in Grandpa's worn green rocking chair. I remember wanting to tell him to stop.

"Um hum, yes, well, I'm sure your daddy would have been proud, Larry," Grandma said, shaken, tired, and ever making up stories. Grandpa had never been proud of Uncle Larry.

"Yeah, he surely would have," Uncle Larry said. "He (sniff, cough) sh-sh-surely would have been proud, M-m-m-a-mama."

I haven't seen such a large man hunch over like that and shake. And I haven't heard such a large man let out the kinds of blubbery sounds that came from the deepest pit of a his stomach. But there he was, Uncle Larry, blubbering, and for a minute he looked honest as he gripped his greased, stringy hair between his fingers and dug his elbows into his knees. Dimples and dikes poxed his cheeks, his face tightening as he cried. He looked so uncomfortable, like his body couldn't fit him anymore and his clothes couldn't fit his body. Something was going to have to give because he couldn't keep himself together much longer. His head was out-growing his hair at the top, his hands seemed too bloated to make a fist, like a blown-up rubber glove, and the bottom of his pants, stretched and frayed, came up to the middle of his calves when he sat there, hunched over.

I left Grandma and Uncle Larry sitting in the living room, and I went into my room to take off my funeral clothes. I never liked wearing black. It reminded me of things. And even though they were more of a peach color earlier that day, my underwear even looked black. So I stood in my room, naked, picking lint from my skin, until I put on some new underwear. Then, I stood in my new ones looking into the long mirror nailed on my closet door.

Depending on the position I take in front of that mirror, certain parts of my body will stretch out or sink in. I tried to poke out my belly like Uncle Larry's to see what it was like. But my stomach wouldn't go out that far (unless I leaned sideways and bent my knees).

When I came back out of my room in a t-shirt and shorts, I saw Uncle Larry, red in the face, beating and pulling on the one window that was nailed shut. Trying to open it. Cursing Grandpa for never having fixed it.

❋

There's a birch tree in our front yard, a scraggly tree with its bark curling up and peeling off, like it's bored or something, like my mom's skin. You can see a little of the tree from the nailed window, if you stretch your neck far enough and press your head against the windowpane. It's split in two at the base, each half of the tree getting farther away from the other. I was never able to climb up either side, the one growing towards the shed or the one growing towards the road. I could only sit in-between the two because the branches were too high for me to reach or too soft for me to sit on.

I don't sit in front of the house much anyway. Besides, sometimes that tree makes me sneeze.

Same with pepper, but my mom collects salt and pepper shakers anyway. She arranges them almost everyday, even if it's just to move one in place of another. And they're always kept full, but even when they're full, they're filled. Or checked. By Mom. They sit on a small, water-stained shelf hung in the kitchen, and she has all kinds. Shakers shaped like mushrooms and chefs, dogs and churches, teapots and tomatoes.

*

"How do you fix a broken tomato?

.

.

.

.

.

Tomato paste!"

*

We've had tomatoes ever since I can remember, and I can remember way back when I was four.

Grandma fixes them all sorts of ways: cut up, whole fried, stewed, green, red, yellow, souped, juiced, spotted, salted, dried, drained, and every other way a tomato can be eaten.

She grows them out back. She's got plastic buckets with stakes that she grows them in. Right now, there are five plastic buckets that she has to water and tend to, and they've got tomatoes in them.

Lotsoftomatoesgrowingupandup.

*

Towards the sun I used to look, until one day Grandma told me looking up there was bad for my eyes. It was hard to keep looking anyway. It made me kind of dizzy. But I don't look anymore since I'm scared, now, and besides, I forget to. I used to wonder how I was going to go through the rest of my entire life without ever looking at the sun. It's so big. It's almost always there. Except when it's night and the crickets play on their washboards. That's what Grandpa always said. That the crickets played washboards at night and that's where all their noise came from. I never asked why the crickets played washboards, because Caroline played the clarinet. And she said she plays the clarinet because she likes the sound it makes and the reed tickles her lips. I like her sound better than the crickets.

Caroline's coming over after supper. She said that tonight we'll go catch fireflies and put them in mason jars.

They make good nightlights when you put the jar in your room. Caroline puts her jar on her nightstand and I put mine on my windowsill. If you put grass inside the jar with the fireflies and punch holes in the top, it keeps them alive longer so they can be put out in morning.

Sometimes they die and I feel bad. Sometimes they die and I don't feel bad. They're just bugs. There are so many of them out back that we could scoop them up with a bulldozer and fill the entire house and not be able to tell outside. Still, I guess some things are better left to themselves because, as Grandpa always used to say *the more you know the less you believe.*

Mom is rubbing one of her slippers on her cheek and humming something I can't make out. It's not that the slippers are all that soft, really, only that they were soft once. The part that covers her toes is wool. And the wool was soft once and clean once and curly, but now they're stubbly and worn and brown. I think Mom remembers them. I like to think she remembers the time when they were new.

I'm tired of sitting, and sitting makes me tired. But I'm still here. The sun's gone from the window and almost gone for the day. There's a haze in the room resting on top of the furniture, on mom, on me. Grandma's taking a nap, but she'll be up soon (she always is) to fix potatoes and pork chops for dinner.

*

On certain nights, when the moon is crawling up over the house and when it hits the cinderblocks, the house glows like a giant T.V., a steady glow that doesn't stay long. And on other certain nights, the clouds are low, and the fog rolls and drifts over and tucks into everything. It was on these nights, when the top of the house was all I could see, that I used to run out into the fog and imagine that the house was a ship sinking in a sea. And sometimes I would worry about all the things that would be lost; sometimes I wouldn't worry at all. I would swim in the fog and try to get to the top of the house, get to something high above the water. But every time I swam there, I would arrive at the front porch or at other cinderblock walls under the clouds, under the water.
I would

s

i

n

k

along with the house. And I would grasp for air and sputter and gurgle, and for a moment I would remember the things about myself that I wanted to remember. And for a moment I would die, but not for long. It was all pretend.

About the Author

Krista Creel received her undergraduate degree in creative writing from the University of Memphis and her graduate degree in journalism. She has had short stories and poems published by the Universities of Pennsylvania, Chicago, Johnson & Wales, South Arkansas and Memphis, as well as other independent literary magazines. She lives in rural West Tennessee with her family.

www.ingramcontent.com/pod-product-compliance
Lightning Source LLC
Chambersburg PA
CBHW021023120726
47905CB00009B/3153